Bolton wanted so to pull Clarice against him, to kiss her...

to laugh with her, to claim her and the boy as family. His family.

"We're having a special Independence Day celebration next week," he told Clarice. "Picnic, games, music and so on. Then afterward, we'll go to the fireworks. I'd like you and Trenton to come."

His heart did not begin its painful beat until the words were said. He waited.

Clarice smiled. "We'd love to."

It took every ounce of his willpower to hide his true feelings. His heart felt like a cloud expanding in his chest. Yes. Oh, yes. He closed his eyes briefly in thanks, then got a hold on himself.

She had said yes to a picnic, nothing more. But it was a start, wasn't it?

Dear Reader,

This month we have a wonderful lineup of books for you—romantic reading that's sure to take the chill out of these cool winter nights.

What happens when two precocious kids advertise for a new father—and a new husband—for their mom? The answer to that question and *much* more can be found in the delightful *Help Wanted: Daddy* by Carolyn Monroe. This next book in our FABULOUS FATHERS series is filled with love, laughter and larger-than-life hero Boone Shelton—a truly irresistible candidate for fatherhood.

We're also very pleased to present Diana Palmer's latest Romance, *King's Ransom*. A spirited heroine and a royal hero marry first and find love later in this exciting and passionate story. We know you won't want to miss it.

Don't forget to visit that charming midwestern town, Duncan, Oklahoma, in *A Wife Worth Waiting For,* the conclusion to Arlene James's THIS SIDE OF HEAVEN trilogy. Bolton Charles, who has appeared in earlier titles, finally meets his match in Clarice Revere. But can Bolton convince her that he's unlike the domineering men in her past?

Rounding out the list, Joan Smith's *Poor Little Rich Girl* is a breezy, romantic treat. And Kari Sutherland makes a welcome return with *Heartfire, Homefire*. We are also proud to present the debut of a brand-new author in Romance, Charlotte Moore with *Not the Marrying Kind*. When the notorious Beth Haggerty returns to her hometown, she succeeds in stirring up just as much gossip as always—and just as much longing in the heart of Deputy Sheriff Raymond Hawk.

In the months ahead, there are more wonderful romances coming your way by authors such as Annette Broadrick, Elizabeth August, Marie Ferrarella, Carla Cassidy and many more. Please write to us with your comments and suggestions. We take your opinions to heart.

Happy reading,

Anne Canadeo
Senior Editor

A WIFE WORTH WAITING FOR

Arlene James

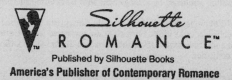

Silhouette
R O M A N C E™
Published by Silhouette Books
America's Publisher of Contemporary Romance

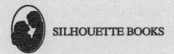

SILHOUETTE BOOKS

ISBN 0-373-08974-0

A WIFE WORTH WAITING FOR

Printed in U.S.A.

ARLENE JAMES

grew up in Oklahoma and has lived all over the South. In 1976 she married "the most romantic man in the world." The author enjoys traveling with her husband, but writing has always been her chief pastime.

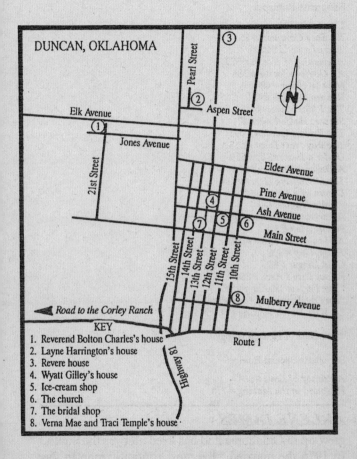

DUNCAN, OKLAHOMA

Pearl Street

③

② Aspen Street

N

Elk Avenue

① Jones Avenue

21st Street

Elder Avenue

Pine Avenue

④ Ash Avenue

⑦ ⑤ ⑥ Main Street

15th Street
14th Street
13th Street
12th Street
11th Street
10th Street

⑧ Mulberry Avenue

◀ Road to the Corley Ranch

KEY

Route 1

Highway 81

1. Reverend Bolton Charles's house
2. Layne Harrington's house
3. Revere house
4. Wyatt Gilley's house
5. Ice-cream shop
6. The church
7. The bridal shop
8. Verna Mae and Traci Temple's house

Chapter One

It was a summons, plain and simple. Bolton chuckled and looked again at the folded sheet of stationery, very white against the green blotter on his desk. The shaky slashes of black ink revealed a bold hand infirmed by age and illness, but the wording was that of a self-assured despot. The Reverend Bolton Charles would please present himself at Revere House the following morning at the hour of eleven to discuss a matter of grave importance. His promptness was appreciated—and taken for granted. He would go, of course. Those of his profession could not afford to look askance at the manner in which a need for aid was presented, however high-handed the presentation. The only question in his mind was what he could do for Wallis Revere. Revere had made it plain in the past that Bolton's "interference" was not wanted. Bolton couldn't help wondering what had happened to change that. As he considered the possibilities, he sobered.

Wallis Revere was seventy-three years old, his birthday falling sometime in February. Bolton knew this because, as a minister, it was his practice to mark the birthdays of each and every one of his church members, whether they participated in the function of the church or not, and Wallis Revere did not. Actually, Carol, the reverend's late wife, had started the practice, and it was one of her many projects that he had struggled to continue during the two years and four months since her death.

Two years, four months, one week and two days. He could quickly figure the hours and minutes, as well, if he would allow himself the luxury of maudlin reflection. But he would not. Carol was gone. His own life went on. God's ways were often mysterious, and his own faith was such that he needed no other explanation for the single most devastating event of his life. His wife had died of cancer. He missed her horribly, and yet what he missed most these days was having someone beside him, someone sharing his life, not Carol herself precisely, but *someone.* Someone to love— he wanted someone to love. A woman. He was man enough, human enough, to admit that he wanted, needed a woman, his own woman. God had designed men and women to want and need and love one another. He never ceased to marvel at that fact. *Mysterious ways,* he reminded himself, and resolutely turned his thoughts back to work.

Revere was elderly, ailing from some sort of degenerative bone disease, and stubbornly reclusive. He had not welcomed the three previous calls that Bolton had dutifully paid him. In fact, Revere had been barely civil on those past occasions, dismissing the minister quite firmly in the end. Nevertheless, he had continued his generous monthly monetary contributions to the church's treasury—and now it appeared that the old boy was ready to extract his money's worth from the minister whose comfortable salary he helped to provide. It was, of course, the very sort of thing that Bolton Charles was paid to do. Visit the infirm and elderly, render aid to the needy, comfort, advise, counsel, exhort, pray... organize, oversee, encourage, teach, preach, intercede, introduce, support, defend... The list was endless, but they were all duties, each and every one, for which he was *called* much more than *hired,* and for that reason he would clear his schedule and appear at Revere House at precisely eleven the next morning. He would have gone even if Revere previously had tossed him out on his backside, revoked his church membership and demanded a refund of his tithes. Bolton's reasons were simple. He was a man of God, a minister, sworn to aid the needy in body and soul. He considered that no greater calling existed, and he was thankful beyond words that it was his own. But that moved him no closer to divining Wallis Revere's problem.

Might not the old boy have developed a concern for his soul? The dying often did, and it certainly was not beyond the realm of possibility that the man was dying. Bolton hoped it was not so. A minister's job was inexorably coiled up with death, and while his personal belief in heaven was firm, dealing with death and dying and its aftermath for the living was a decidedly unpleasant business. But one he did well, especially after his own personal experience in that area. He had never truly understood the matter of comfort for the bereaved or how to give it until Carol had left him. He wondered who, if anyone, would grieve Wallis Revere.

By eleven the next morning, he had satisfied himself somewhat on that question. A discreet conversation with his secretary, Cora Beemis, had elicited the nearly forgotten intelligence that the Revere family consisted of Wallis, a young grandson and a daughter-in-law, the widow of Revere's son and only child, who had died some years previously in a riding accident. Neither the daughter-in-law nor the grand-

son were members of the congregation, which, coupled with
Revere's stubborn reclusiveness, explained why Bolton knew
little of them. He was relieved, however, just to know that
they existed. It was the thought of them that occupied his
mind as he turned his conservative four-door sedan through
the brick columns flanking the broad drive of the Revere
estate.

Estate was the only word for the Revere place. It was
nestled, as much as a three-story Georgian-style colon-
naded house with various outbuildings could be nestled, in
a gentle, shady hollow on the northern edge of the Duncan
city limits. The site itself was atypical of this section of
Oklahoma, which tended to consist of rolling fields spliced
with low, eroded, red-orange cliffs sparsely scattered with
spindly post oak, willow and mesquite. The only significant tree growth seemed to be restricted to the areas surrounding the creeks, lakes and ponds that dotted this south
central portion of the state. But Wallis Revere had found—
or created—a cool, leafy vale all his own, as cool, anyway,
as an Oklahoma morning in a new June could get. The ra-
dio had reported only minutes earlier that the temperature
was eighty-four degrees and climbing. It would break ninety
before the day was done, and soon summer would be upon
them with a vengeance.

Bolton parked the car in a shady spot on the circular drive
and lowered the window several inches before getting out.
The place was quiet except for the rustle of leaves and the
gentle chirping of unseen birds. A fat blond cat with a single ear and a patchwork of scars on one flank ambled up the
brick walk with dignified unconcern. Bolton followed it to
the door, feeling absurdly as if he ought to speak.

"Nice day for a stroll, isn't it?"

The cat twitched its single ear as if in dismissal and
hopped up onto the doorstep, twisting itself sinuously

around the base of a big clay pot containing a small tree and a lot of drooping ivy. Bolton stepped up behind the cat and pressed the doorbell button. Almost instantly the paneled door opened and a plump, smiling Mexican woman appeared. She was wearing a simple shirtwaist dress, a pristine white apron and clunky black shoes. Her hairline was streaked with gray, but the long ponytail draped over one shoulder was black as ink. Her slender black eyebrows went up.

"Preacher?" she asked in heavily accented English.

Bolton nodded. "Reverend Charles. And you are?"

"Teresa."

"Nice to meet you, Teresa."

She giggled and beckoned with a plump, chapped hand for him to follow. "Meester Wallis is in de study," she informed him, leading him across the foyer and down a long, dark hall flanking the stairwell. She opened a door and stepped aside.

Bolton gave her a truncated bow and a smile. "Thank you, Teresa."

She giggled again and hurried away. Bolton stepped into the dark, stuffy room.

Wallis Revere was seated in his wheelchair before a cold fireplace. "Close the door," he ordered summarily.

Bolton complied. So much for the niceties of polite greetings and small talk. He walked farther into the room and let his gaze take in the old man glaring up at him with piercing eyes. Revere seemed not to have changed so much as a cell. His hair, though white, was lushly thick and meticulously groomed. His long, narrow face was scored and sunken, yet somehow vital, despite the pallor of his skin, the razor thinness of his nose and the weight of bushy white brows that seemed drawn together in a permanent scowl. Perhaps that face owed its vitality to his mouth, which was wide and full-lipped. Yes, the mouth—and the eyes, which were as bright and vibrant a green as any emerald.

Bolton took in the burgundy cardigan, the soft gray shirt and the carefully knotted tie, the starched creases of charcoal slacks, coordinated argyles and black wingtips and decided that death was not yet knocking at this particular door. Relieved, he allowed himself to relax and give rein to his curiosity. "How can I help you, Wallis?"

Revere leaned back in his chair. He was a tall, thin man with big feet and hands, now gnarled and weak but still commanding. He seemed to be trying to satisfy himself on some private point, then having done so, nodded. "Sit down, Reverend. I don't like to ask favors of anyone I have to look up to."

Bolton tried not to show his surprise as he crossed to a comfortable leather wing chair and folded himself into it. Favors? Since when did Wallis Revere ever ask favors of anyone? Bolton folded his hands and leaned forward, indicating his willingness to listen.

Wallis Revere grimaced. "What I wouldn't give for arms and legs that work as they're supposed to," he said, then lifted his chin. "I have a job for a man, a *real* man, not some namby-pamby afraid of his own shadow. Mind you, I don't want a bully, but I need a man of strong character and deep conviction. I think you're that man."

Bolton couldn't have contained his surprise this time if he'd tried. "Well, thank you."

Revere lifted a gnarled hand dismissively. "I've met a good many ministers in my day. Some are sensitive to the point of being effeminate and so other-worldly, they're of no use in this one. I judge you the exception, and that's why I've asked you here."

Bolton waited, sure more was to come.

Wallis Revere smiled in a smug, self-satisfied manner and got down to it. "I have an eight-year-old grandson, soon to be nine. His father got himself killed over five years ago. Pulled a damn fool stunt on a horse and got his neck broke. In all the time since, there have been just his mother and I, for all the good I am to him. He needs the company and influence of a whole man, someone strong but respectful, someone who knows his duty and doesn't shirk it."

Why, the old crank was looking for a surrogate father for the boy! Bolton lifted both slender, coffee-black brows, torn between amusement and offense. Clearly Revere thought him man enough for the job, but Bolton suspected Revere considered him "manageable" as well. Perhaps it was time to disabuse the old boy. "I think playing dad to a boy I've never even met is stretching the description of my 'duties' pretty thin. I'm a minister, not a foster parent."

Revere screwed up his face in an expression of impatience. "Exactly so. You're a minister, and *I* am one of your flock. You won't refuse a call for help from one of your own. I know you better than that. Besides, the boy needs you. No one's asking you to adopt him. Just spend time with him, let him see how you handle yourself. Now, is that too much to ask?"

Bolton frowned. It was a lot to ask, but too much? Well, he supposed that depended on what he was dealing with here. Any grandson of Wallis Revere's was bound to be a snotty little prince—unless, of course, the good Lord had seen fit to tweak old Wallis's pride. It was just possible the boy was somehow a disappointment to the old man. Perhaps he lacked the natural arrogance of a Revere. Maybe he was too "other-worldly" for his grandfather's tastes. And maybe it was something else altogether. Maybe the kid just needed someone to toss a ball around with him. Bolton crossed his legs and pinched the crease of his navy slacks just

above the knee, thinking. Finally he looked up. "I'll have
to meet the boy before I can make a decision," he stated
evenly.

Wallis nodded and rolled his chair backward. Reaching
around the end of the fireplace, he pressed a buzzer bar
fastened to the wall. Half a minute later, Teresa opened the
door.

"Do you want me, Meester Wallis?"

"Bring Trent in right away."

The woman nodded and hurriedly left them. During her
absence, Wallis condescended to make small talk, com-
menting on the weather and the state of the economy before turning the conversation back to his grandson. The boy
had just finished second grade, was an exceptional reader
and a whiz at math. He was learning to play the piano and
roller skate. He wrestled and held the title in his league's
weight class. Revere's pride in the boy was evident in the
careless manner in which he revealed all this. Bolton didn't
know what to expect. When the door opened a second time,
he sat forward, blatantly curious.

A little boy with light brown hair and his grandfather's
vibrant green eyes walked into the room. He was your average kid, dressed in blue-jean shorts with neatly rolled cuffs
and an oversize T-shirt bearing the logo of a professional
basketball team. He wore a wristwatch and expensive high-
top athletic shoes with black socks. His thick, straight, light
brown hair had been cut in a modishly conservative style:
very, very short in back, considerably longer on the top and
sides. It showed signs of having once been parted but now
fell forward in a thatch of bangs that covered one eyebrow.
He was taller and bigger than average, more physically mature in some ways than any other eight-year-olds Bolton had
known. Otherwise, he was just an average kid. His face was
yet too round to display any significant bone structure. His

fingernails were too short, as if they'd been bitten back. He had a nasty scrape just below one knee. Wallis beckoned to him.

"Come here, Trent, and meet Reverend Charles."

The boy walked forward without hesitation and offered the reverend a noticeably grimy hand. Bolton swamped it with his own, pleasantly surprised by the strength in the boy's grip. "How do you do, sir?"

"Very well, thank you. And you, Trent? I have the feeling we took you away from something interesting."

The boy nodded engagingly. He was a very self-possessed sort and rather solemn. "I was checking my traps," he revealed.

Wallis chuckled. "We've a skunk somewhere hereabouts, and I've given orders that it's to be shot at first opportunity. Trent disagrees with my solution to the problem. He thinks he can trap the critter and make a friend of it."

Bolton disciplined a smile. "Aside from the obvious problem," he said, addressing Trent, "have you considered the possibility that the skunk could carry rabies?"

The boy's chin went up a fraction of an inch. "I wasn't going to let it bite me," he said, very matter-of-fact.

Bolton regrouped quickly. "Of course not. I was thinking more of the other animals a rabid skunk could infect, like that old battle-scarred cat I met outside."

"General," the boy murmured, obviously thinking.

"I beg your pardon?"

Trent looked mildly confused for a moment. "Oh. His name is General. General Tom."

"I like that," Bolton said. "It suits him."

"He's not a very nice old cat," Trent said. "If you pet him, he'll hang his claws in you. But I like him anyway."

"He kind of makes you respect him, doesn't he?" Bolton commented.

The boy looked at him consideringly. He was forming an opinion. Bolton believed it would be a favorable one. Apparently, so did Wallis, and that was what seemed to matter to the old man. "You can get back to your traps now, Trent," Wallis said dismissively.

His high-handedness suddenly irritated Bolton immensely. Before he could stop himself, he caught hold of the boy's hands. "Not just yet. I'd like to ask you a few questions, Trent."

The boy tensed but did not object. "What?"

"What are your favorite things to do?"

Trent shrugged. "Video games. Reading. Movies. Cartoons. I like to draw sometimes."

All solitary amusements. "Who's your very best friend?" Bolton asked.

Again the boy seemed confused. He thought a long time, then slid a wary glance toward his grandfather. "Denny Carter, I guess." The old man scowled. Trent rushed on. "He's older than me but not bigger, and he's the only one who can beat me wrestling."

"You like him, do you?" Bolton pressed.

Trent held his gaze for a long moment. "Like General Tom," he said finally.

"You respect him, then," Bolton mused. "And does he like you?"

Trent's gaze wavered. He fortified it. "He likes being able to beat me."

Bolton wondered what the answer would be if he asked Trent if he *let* Denny Carter beat him at wrestling. He glimpsed something unsettling behind that calm gaze, as if the boy was terrified that he would ask that very question. Bolton took pity on him and clapped his hand over his shoulder, putting on a smile of satisfaction. "Anybody would like you, Trent," he said. "I certainly do."

The kid's relief was palpable, though not evident. "Thank you. It was very nice meeting you, sir."

"It was very nice meeting you, too, Trent." Bolton put his hand on the boy's back, turned him toward the door and gave him a little shove. He fled with all the enthusiasm of every kid escaping the confusing presence of adults. When he was gone, Bolton looked at Revere. The old man was frowning, but he quickly smiled. Bolton doubted Wallis Revere had the least concern over his grandson's lamentable lack of friends his own age, not that it mattered. "He's a fine boy," Bolton said. "I'll like spending time with him."

Triumph infused the old man with an almost physical power. "Wonderful. I'll have my daughter-in-law bring him around tomorrow for a get-acquainted session."

Daughter-in-law. Trent's mother. Bolton cocked his head. "I trust she approves of this arrangement."

The old man dismissed that concern with a wave of his hand. "Why shouldn't she?"

Bolton bit his tongue. *High-handed* was an understatement where Wallis Revere was concerned. He got to his feet, aware that his temper had been stirred and unwilling to allow it free rein. "I'm afraid I won't be available until about four o'clock," he said firmly. "I'll expect them then."

Revere nodded. "Four o'clock it is." He extended his hand, neck craned at what seemed an uncomfortable angle.

Bolton took it, careful to keep his grip light. He knew without a doubt that he wasn't about to hear an expression of Revere's gratitude. That old despot didn't know the meaning of the word. But it didn't matter. Whatever he did, and he wasn't at all certain now what that would be, it would be for the boy's sake, regardless of the grandfather's intent. He would make his decision after speaking with the boy's mother and not before. As he saw it, the boy's mother was the authority on the boy's welfare and his duty was to the boy rather than the old man. That thought gave Bolton immense satisfaction, and he didn't bother to chastise himself for enjoying it while he shook the old man's trembling hand.

Bolton let himself out after voicing the opinion that Teresa had been bothered enough for one morning. His stomach was telling him that it was almost lunchtime, and as he got into his car he decided that he would pick up a bite to eat on his way back to the church. He usually ate carry-in with Cora, but Cora was lunching with her daughter and grandchildren that day, so it would be a solitary meal, as so many of his meals were.

He paused a moment at the gates of the Revere estate, pondering this new situation. He'd been called upon in many ways over the years, but he'd never been asked to play surrogate father. It was ironic in a way. He'd expected to be enjoying the real thing by now. Yet, for some reason, God had seen fit to deny him that privilege—not that it was too late by any means. He was only thirty-seven, and he had always intended to marry again; during those final weeks before the cancer had taken her, Carol had insisted that he must. The problem was that he just hadn't found the right woman yet. He had thought for a short time last summer that he was on the right track, but the young lady in question had developed interests in another area. He smiled as he thought about the Gilleys. How he envied Wyatt his family, twin boys and a lovely wife already big with another of Wyatt's children. It was a good thing he also liked Wyatt Gilley immensely or their relationship could be strained.

As it was, he counted the Gilleys among his closest friends. Wyatt was a bit rough around the edges, but that was one of the things Bolton liked best about him. Wyatt was honest. He didn't put his "Sunday face" on just because the preacher was around. In fact, Bolton doubted Wyatt even had a "Sunday face." That made it very easy to relax around the man. Wyatt was good for him.

Maybe, if it came about, this arrangement with Trent Revere would be a good thing for him, too. He was a busy man, but he was also a lonely man in many ways. Trent was likely to liven things up a bit. What that boy needed most was somebody to play with him, somebody who would let him be a kid just for the sheer joy of it, somebody who could make him feel safe and protected and carefree. Unless Bolton's judgment was skewed, the boy needed him. Maybe they needed each other. The kid seemed as lonely as he was. It occurred to him for the first time to wonder what Trent's mother was like. Wallis had hardly mentioned her, and neither had Trent, though he hadn't really had any opportunity. Bolton wondered briefly how it was that he had never met the woman. It was odd that she had never attended the services at his church. Perhaps she was of a different religious persuasion. If so, would she object to his spending time with her son? He suddenly hoped that was not the case. He liked that little boy. He was rather surprised to find how much he was looking forward to their first outing.

A light tap sounded on his office door at precisely four o'clock. Bolton put away the sermon notes he had been jotting down and rose to walk around his desk and lounge upon its corner.

"Come in."

The door opened and a small, pretty female walked through. Bolton came instantly to his feet, taken off guard by the delicate creature before him. Her wispy blond bangs hung in her eyes. The remainder, cropped at chin length,

swirled around her head in charming disarray. Then she
lifted her hands and swept the whole of it back from her
face; it fell forward again in soft wings that revealed the
precise, sophisticated cut. She smiled politely, the softness
of her full mouth belied by the sharpness of large, tilted,
moss-green eyes set deeply beneath straight, delicate brows.
Her nose, though small, was finely cut. Her chin, gently
pointed, gave way to the roundness of high-boned cheeks,
lending her face the piquant shape of a heart. She straightened the ribbed bottom of the sleeveless, periwinkle-blue
knit top she wore with a matching pleated skirt. A single
pearl at each earlobe was the only jewelry she wore. Bolton
noticed, with interest, that she was not wearing a wedding
ring.

She held out a dainty hand with manicured nails painted
a soft shell pink. "Reverend Charles, I am Clarice Revere."

"I assumed as much." He smiled, very conscious of the
way his hand literally swallowed hers. Hers was cool, almost weightless, making him very aware of the heat and
heaviness of his own. There was something very sensuous
about that. He cleared his throat, as if that would clear away
uncomfortable thoughts. "Ah, where is Trent? I thought he
would be with you."

Her smile was thin, rueful. "Yes, Wallis did intend that,
but my father-in-law sometimes forgets that Trenton has a
mother who does not like to shirk her responsibilities. I felt
we should talk, you and I, before *I* decide whether or not
this notion of Wallis's is a good idea."

Well, this was a surprise. Here was a female, small and
cool and delicate, whom Wallis Revere had not succeeded
in cowing despite years of undoubted effort. The lady possessed hidden strength. Bolton liked that. His grip tightened on her hand. Only then did he realize that he still held

it. He let it go, forcing himself not to snatch his own hand back as if hers was a hot potato, and offered her a chair. Then, in a deliberate effort to put distance between them, he went back to his place behind the desk.

When they were both comfortably settled, he began. "What would you like to know, Mrs. Revere?"

She grimaced. "Clarice, please. In my mind, Mrs. Revere is still my late mother-in-law."

He nodded, ridiculously pleased. "A fine woman, I understand."

"A doormat," she said bluntly, then grimaced again. "Forgive me. I'm afraid cynicism is a necessity in my present circumstance. Wallis is a terribly controlling man. I find I must remind myself at every turn not to knuckle under."

"Which is what she did?" he asked gently.

Clarice Revere took a deep breath, as if immensely relieved to find that he understood. "Yes, and what I did for a long time, too."

He templed his fingers. "I gather this visit has something to do with not 'knuckling under' again."

Her smile was self-deprecating this time. "You're a very perceptive man, Reverend."

He bit back the temptation to offer her his given name, reminding himself that he was functioning here as a professional. "I don't know Wallis well," he said carefully, "but well enough."

She laughed, the sound rich and clear and bright. "I think he was right in this instance."

"About?"

"You," she said. "About you being a good influence for my son."

His pleasure at that was inordinate—and a little dangerous. Only with great effort did he manage to keep his manner one of relaxed professionalism. "Thank you. I look forward to spending time with Trent. Maybe you could give me some idea what he would like to do. His own list of favorite activities were rather solitary exercises.''

She frowned, nodding. ''I am aware of that fact,'' she said. Then she sighed and leaned forward in the manner of one about to confide a personal secret. ''I should explain something to you, Reverend Charles. This determination of mine not to let Wallis control our lives is fairly new. You see, when you're lost and alone and responsible for a young child, it's horribly easy to let someone else take care of you, and when that someone is a man like Wallis Revere, well, you find yourself being taken over completely. You start to lose yourself, and when that happens, you start to lose even the will to go on. I let that happen to myself a long time ago, but when I realized that it was happening to my son, too...'' She lifted her chin. ''I'm fighting him every way I know how, and I'm trying so hard to fight smart, to pick my battles and approach them from the position of greatest strength. But it isn't easy. I have to weigh every situation carefully and be absolutely certain that if I take a position opposite Wallis that it is because it is the *right* thing to do. Do you understand what I'm trying to say?''

He stifled the very inappropriate impulse to applaud the woman! Instead, he sat forward, forearms aligned atop the blotter on his desk, and mentally tamped down the absurd elation he was feeling. ''I not only understand,'' he said carefully, ''I also approve, for what that's worth.''

The smile she presented him this time was so brilliant, it almost left him gasping. ''It's worth a great deal!'' she told him. ''It means I can trust you to consider my wishes over those of my father-in-law should the two conflict.''

He was a little shocked. ''But that goes without saying. You are, after all, the boy's mother.''

He thought he saw the shimmer of tears in her eyes before she dropped her gaze to her lap, but when she lifted her head abruptly a moment later, she was very much in control of herself. She crossed her slender legs at the knee, tugging gently at the hem of her skirt. He found it an oddly provocative gesture and shifted his gaze away.

"I'm a little surprised at how this has gone," she said. "I wanted to be honest with you, and you've made that very easy. Now I must ask that you be honest with me."

He sat back again, liking her more and more. "By all means."

She sat forward, her whole posture suddenly intense. "Were you coerced into this *arrangement* with my son? Isn't it an inconvenience to be saddled with someone else's little boy? Wouldn't you rather *not* go through with it?"

Bolton couldn't help grinning. "No. In fact, I'm looking forward to it. Very much."

She seemed pleased, *very* pleased. She relaxed. Her face softened, her eyes seeming to grow quite large and doelike. "Oh, how easy you make it for me. I can't tell you how grateful I am! Trenton really does need a man's guidance, Reverend Charles, and I couldn't be more pleased with my father-in-law's choice. But you mustn't let us become a nuisance. Promise me that you won't let us take unreasonable advantage of your time or generosity."

Us. A wave of heat spread through the reverend, at once oddly familiar and utterly foreign. He heard himself saying, "I promise, provided you'll call me Bolton."

She gave him that brilliant smile again. It forced him to gulp down a sudden lump in his throat.

"Of course," she said, "and you must call me Clarice." Then, getting to her feet, she held out her hand again. "Thank you, Bolton, for everything."

He scrambled up and around the desk, grasping her fingertips. "Uh, about Trent... that is, your suggestions for activities of interest to... us, him... and me, that is."

She laughed at him. It was a most companionable laugh, almost affectionate. "I'm sure you'll do very well in that area all on your own. Why don't we take a clue from Wallis in this instance? Why don't I bring Trenton around for a short visit, and the two of you can decide how you want to begin. All right?"

He nodded, feeling patently ridiculous for having babbled so. "Fine. This evening perhaps? Or tomorrow morning. Whatever is most convenient."

"We are completely at your disposal. Choose a time."

He couldn't think for the life of him. Finally he just snatched a time out of thin air. "Nine-thirty."

She shook his hand. "Nine-thirty tomorrow morning it is."

Tomorrow morning. Of course. Nine-thirty at night would hardly be the time to begin such a project. "Right," he said, hoping he didn't sound like the idiot he felt at the moment.

She smiled at him benignly. "I'll see you tomorrow then."

"Right. I mean, yes. Tomorrow, definitely."

"At nine-thirty."

"Ri—uh, uh-huh." He was starting to sound like a broken record, for pity's sake!

She gently extracted her hand from his and left, that smile upon her face.

Bolton sank down upon the corner of his desk, mind awhirl. Well. He felt as if he'd been hit between the eyes. She was not at all what he'd expected. This woman was no cipher, no colorless, defeated little wren. She was gentle, yes, and sensitive—even delicate—yet intelligence and determination had lit a bright spark of vivacity in her—and struck sparks off him. Oh, yes, sparks were flying everywhere. He laughed aloud, eager to see her again, to feel those sparks again, which he would do at nine-thirty the next morning. Suddenly he smacked himself in the forehead with the flat of his hand. Quickly he leaned across the desk and slapped the button on his intercom machine.

"Cora?"

"Yeah?"

"Do I have anything scheduled for nine-thirty tomorrow morning?"

"Tomorrow?"

"Nine-thirty tomorrow morning," he repeated forcefully.

A lengthy silence followed, then, "Hey, Bolt, tomorrow's Saturday."

Saturday! He gaped, then he snapped off the machine and started to laugh. Saturday. Apparently his mind had gone out to lunch the moment Clarice Revere had walked through the door! Could it be, he wondered, that Wallis Revere, of all people, had actually introduced him, finally, to *the* woman his own beloved Carol had promised him existed. If so, that old saw about God working in mysterious ways had just proven a serious understatement. Why, the mind boggled. He shook his head. Wallis Revere. Miracles, apparently, did still happen.

Chapter Two

He was waiting in the outer office when they arrived, long legs crossed at the ankles as he leaned against the corner of his secretary's desk. He looked uncommonly handsome and surprisingly at ease in fringed loafers, crisp white jeans and a sky-blue polo shirt. His short, dark hair was combed casually to one side from a straight part, and his mouth was curved upward in a welcoming smile that deserved a like response. She could not deny the urge to give it to him, and so moments later found herself standing in the middle of the floor grinning like an idiot while his dark winged brows slowly lifted. The realization brought on a fit of giggles, which she stifled with less than complete success. Trenton, solemn little man that he was, stared up at her with undisguised curiosity. The look on his face said it all: his mother never giggled. Clarice cleared her throat and schooled her expression.

"Reverend Charles," she said decorously.

Those winged brows pulled down into a frown. "I thought we had agreed on given names."

And so they had. Whatever was wrong with her? "Yes, of course. Well then, Bolton, I believe you've met my son, Trent."

"Indeed I have." He straightened and stepped forward, bending slightly to offer his hand to the boy. "How are you this morning, Trent?"

Obediently, Trent shook hands. "Fine, sir, thank you."

The reverend folded his arms thoughtfully. "You have excellent manners, young man. Do you think we could dispose of them in favor of something as mundane as, say, friendship?"

The boy merely stared at the tall, dark man before him, then, ever so slowly, he turned a questioning gaze up at his mother. Clarice smiled. Why not? Heaven knew her little boy seldomly had opportunity to be just that, a little boy. Why did she think this man could teach her son how to be a child? Trent turned his attention back to the reverend, his expression as inscrutable as usual, and slowly nodded.

Bolton Charles ruffled the boy's hair. "Okay, now, buddy, here's the deal. When it's just you and me or maybe you and me and your mom, I'd like you to call me Bolton. That all right with you?"

Trent screwed up one eye and chewed one corner of his mouth in his typical expression of engrossing thought. Clarice smoothed a hand through his hair, repairing the damage done earlier and fixing this moment in her mind. He was such an endearing little boy. So bright, so beautiful, so determined to be all that he was expected to be—and with such conflicting expectations! Wallis wanted a carbon copy of the son he had lost, who in turn had been meant to be a carbon copy of himself, while she wanted only for her son to discover who and what he was. She was under no illusions about Wallis's motives in setting up this arrangement between Bolton Charles and her son. His goal, ultimately, was to remove Trenton as much as possible from her influence. What Wallis failed to consider was that by bringing in Bolton to monopolize the boy's time, he also removed his grandson from his *own* influence. She dropped her hands to her son's narrow shoulders, prompting him to answer the reverend's question. Obediently, Trenton complied.

"I think I'll call you Bolt," he announced firmly.

The reverend blinked, clearly taken aback, but then a hand came out to stroke his chin and a grin slowly stretched his mouth into a broad curve. "All right, if you like."

Trenton shrugged, unconcerned. "I do," he said ingenuously. "It fits you."

"Does it now?"

"Mmm-hmm. 'Sides, I like having my own names for people," Trent admitted.

Bolton laughed. "All right. Bolt it is. Now suppose you tell me what you prefer to be called."

The reply was immediate. "Trent."

"Not Trenton?" the reverend asked, glancing at Clarice.

The boy tilted his head back and sent a look of his own up at his mother. Clarice's heart seemed to expand to fill her entire chest as she recognized the love and trust shining in her son's eyes. But there was more. In that look was also the desire to protect, and it made her wince inwardly. How had she let this happen? What other eight-year-old bore the burden of protecting his mother? Mothers were supposed to protect their children, not vice versa. Silently she promised her son that things were going to change, and her hands tightened commensurately upon his shoulders. That seemed to satisfy something in her son, for he then swung his gaze around to the reverend.

"Trenton is the name my mother calls me," he said. He might as well have added that she was the only one allowed to do so.

Bolton lifted his gaze to Clarice's, but she couldn't interpret the expression there. "Good enough," he said quietly, and his eyes held hers a moment longer before he dropped them once more to the boy. "Well, Trent, I had in mind to toss around a baseball this morning. Want to join me?"

Clarice knew that in this instance the inscrutable look upon her son's face meant he had misgivings that he was trying to hide.

"I don't know if I'd like it," he said bluntly. What he meant was that he hadn't ever done it before.

The message, thankfully, did not escape Bolton Charles. He shrugged. "Why don't we give it a try? If we're not any good at it, we'll do something else."

Trenton screwed up that eye again, then briskly nodded.

Bolton clapped him on the shoulder. "Great!" He pointed toward the door in the far wall. "There are two gloves and a ball waiting on a black chair inside my office. If you'll get them, I'll just have a word with your mom."

Trent flipped his mother a look and departed. Clarice watched him go through the door then turned her attention to Bolton Charles. "You handled that well," she said lightly.

He smiled. "I had a long talk with my secretary yesterday. She has two grandchildren. They're younger than Trent, I'm afraid, but since she raised three children of her own, two of them sons, she was able to give me a few insights. Her best advice, I think, was to share things I enjoy with Trent."

"And you enjoy baseball," Clarice surmised.

"When I have the chance," he confirmed, "which isn't often."

She couldn't resist the urge to tease him. "Did you play baseball in high school, *Bolt?*"

He grinned at her. "And college."

That surprised her. "Really? Then you must be pretty good."

"Actually, I *was* good, past tense. I even considered, briefly, playing pro ball."

"What happened?" she asked, her curiosity piqued.

His gaze locked with hers. "Just what was supposed to happen," he told her evenly. "I graduated college and went on to seminary."

"Oh." Of course. What a foolish question. She felt heat rising in her cheeks.

He laughed easily. "Why is it that people seem to think the ministry is foisted on hapless fellows with no particular talent for anything else?"

"I don't know," she said, not quite able to meet his gaze again. "Maybe because it seems such a difficult, thankless job."

"But it isn't," he protested. "You don't see the bank president being asked to toss a ball around with a kid, do you?"

She smiled. "No, I guess not."

Trent reappeared then with the gloves and ball, which he carried over to Bolton. Bolton picked one much the worse for wear and wiggled his hand into it. He then beamed a bright, happy smile at Clarice. "I rest my case."

She laughed outright. "You've really taken your secretary's advice to heart, haven't you?"

"Absolutely. Now, if you'll excuse us, this glove is begging to be used."

He held it up to Trent's ear as if the boy could really hear it beg. Trent giggled, something so completely out of character for him that Clarice felt a shock of guilt, followed swiftly by a welling of gratitude for this good-looking minister. She wondered if he knew how grateful she was. His smile seemed to say that he understood completely, but suddenly it was she who understood. This was what he meant. This was why the ministry for him could never be just a thankless job. This was what it was all about for him. Such goodness and generosity were awesome and therefore a little frightening—and even a little defeating somehow. She felt suddenly diminished, as if she could not measure up to such a standard of goodness.

"I—I have some errands to do," she mumbled, turning away.

"Fine," he said. "Why don't you meet us back here in a couple of hours? Then, if you have no other plans, maybe we could all go to lunch together?"

That unexpected invitation sent her gaze zipping back around to his, but his expression was bland, almost impersonal. Obviously he was just being nice. He was a nice man, after all. He was a *minister,* for pity's sake. She felt a stab of disappointment. "We'll see," she said softly.

He didn't reply to that, and she hurried away, scolding herself for such perverse emotions. Bolton Charles was a fine man, the sort to help anyone he could. Why should she resent his kindness toward her, especially as she was so willing to accept his kindness toward her son? She pushed the disturbing thoughts away, and knew herself for a coward. She simply could not go on refusing to think about the complications that popped up. Somehow she had to take back control of her own life and her son's, and she couldn't do it by continually sticking her head in the sand. She'd had enough of that.

So then, what was she to do? *Admit you're attracted to that man,* for starters, she told herself. *But realize that his attentions to you are part and parcel of his ministry as he sees it—and nothing more.* But she had to do more than realize that fact; she had also to accept it, weigh her own choices, and decide how to respond to the reverend. Resolutely, she turned the matter over and over in her mind while she went about picking up the clothes from the cleaner, dropping off the vacuum to be repaired and having her hair trimmed.

By the time she returned to meet her son, she had had plenty of good, sober reflection, all done at a distance, and she welcomed the chance to relate to Bolton Charles strictly as a minister. The problem was that the windblown, panting fellow who jogged up to her car and greeted her was very much a man.

His knit polo shirt clung to his body damply, revealing a flat middle, well-developed chest and broad, muscular shoulders. His dark hair had fallen forward in thick, gleaming tendrils, and he tucked his baseball mitt beneath one arm as he freed his hand and pushed his hair back off his forehead. His smile was immediate, welcoming and infectious. Trenton was right behind him and panting just as hard. Apparently they'd had a real workout with the ball gripped in Bolton's right hand.

Bolton laughed as the boy skidded to a halt and collapsed at the edge of the grass. "I think we may have gotten a little carried away," he said to Clarice. "He's got such a strong arm, I forget he's a boy." He looked back at Trenton as he said that last, and the boy beamed. Suddenly Bolton flicked his wrist, and the ball popped up out of his hand. With a grunt, Trenton threw himself backward, his arm flying out, and the ball plopped down into his glove as smoothly as if he'd been ready and waiting. "All right!" Bolton laughed and gave him a thumbs-up before turning back to Clarice. "Kid's got great reflexes, too, and he throws really well on the move. I think you've got a fine, all-around athlete here and you ought to be getting him into Little League sports."

"Well, he does wrestle," she said a bit defensively, and instantly regretted her tone.

He seemed not to notice. "Yes, I know, and he's been very successful at it. I think he can be just as successful at almost any other sport—baseball certainly, football, probably soccer. Basketball, I don't know. Not my game. Anyway, I'll look into it and find out what's available, if you want."

For some reason the very idea sent her into a kind of panic. "Ah, no. I mean, we don't want to be a bother, that is, *more* of a bother."

He flashed her a totally disarming smile. "Don't be silly. I'm having a ball."

At that, Trenton quipped, "A *baseball!*" and let fly a high, wide zinger.

Bolton lurched into action, sprinting across the parking lot to snatch the ball out of the air—barehanded. His glove lay on the asphalt at Clarice's feet, where it had fallen when he'd darted after the ball. Clarice didn't know which was more unbelievable, the satisfied look on Bolton's face when that ball smacked into his bare hands or the force with which her own small son had hurled it heavenward. She was so caught up in those two interconnected mysteries that she at first did not register Trenton's howl of remorse when that ball connected loudly with Bolton's hands. Only when the boy hurtled past her, catapulting himself at Bolton, did she realize anything was wrong.

"I'm sorry!" he cried. "I'm sorry! Your hands!"

Bolton's expression instantly sobered. He went down on his knees, pulling the boy into his arms. "Hey, pal, what's this? You didn't hurt me."

But even Clarice could see that her son's eyes were big and filled with horror. She threw off her shock and started forward, instinctively squelching the desire to run.

Bolton rolled the ball up onto his fingertips and showed it to Trent. "I'm fine," he was saying. "Besides, it wasn't your fault. Nobody made me go after that ball. I knew what I was doing, and I wouldn't have gone after it if I hadn't thought I could catch it safely. Here, I'll show you." He pushed the ball into Trenton's trembling hand and turned his own palm up, his other arm wrapped snugly around the boy's waist. He wiggled his fingers. "See. Right as rain."

In his relief, Trenton slumped against Bolton's shoulder, and Clarice's heart turned over as Bolton gave him a comforting hug. Her steps slowed, and she came to a halt. Bolton obviously had the situation under control, but it was more than that. Suddenly she felt like an interloper. Oddly, Bolton seemed to sense her feelings for he looked up then and smiled at her. His smile had the same comforting aura about it as that hug. She swallowed down a lump that had risen unexpectedly in her throat. Bolton shifted his arm to support the boy, then got to his feet and pushed up to a standing position, lifting the boy with him as easily as if he weighed no more than the ball. He walked toward her, carrying the boy against his shoulder. Trenton's arms were around his neck, and Bolton spoke softly to him as they drew nearer. Trenton nodded and lifted his head, bestowing a smile upon his mother.

"We're ready for lunch, Mom," Bolton announced, "and *we* want hamburgers."

"And fries!" Trenton added happily.

Clarice gulped. "A-all right."

Bolton pushed on toward the car. It was a sleek, two-door white convertible with a candy-apple-red interior, her one attempt at recapturing a carefree youth she'd never actually had. After the impulsive purchase of it, the car had served merely to embarrass her on occasion. She bit her lip, wondering what the good reverend would think of it, and fell in beside him as he strode toward it.

"Uh, you might want to take your own car," she said, but he shook his head.

"Nope. You can drive. I'm tired."

"Oh. Fine." She couldn't help noticing that he didn't *look* tired. He looked like he could carry Trenton downtown and back without breaking into a sweat.

He went around to the passenger side, opened the door, pulled the seat forward and gave Trenton a little shove into the back, claiming the front seat for himself. He slid down into place and buckled himself in. Clarice got in and did likewise, then adjusted the steering wheel to her liking and started the engine.

"I imagine you'd like the air conditioner turned on," she said.

He lifted his arm around the back of her seat and grinned. "Actually, I'd rather put the top down."

"Yeah, Mom, put the top down," Trent echoed.

He liked to ride with the top down, but she usually felt, well, silly. She opened her mouth to say that she'd just come from the beauty shop and didn't want her hair blown around, when Bolton leaned over and crooned plaintively into her ear, "Come on, *Mom,* a little wind and sun never hurt anybody." She closed her mouth and reached up to release the catches that anchored the top to the windshield, then depressed the button that automatically lowered the top. Trenton cheered, Bolton grinned and she felt her own mouth curving into a smile.

"Okay, guys, where do you want to go for those burgers?"

Trenton made a suggestion, but Bolton immediately countered it, reminding the boy that another place had a playground. "Oh, yeah," Trenton said, as if he'd never considered that particular benefit before. Clarice felt a pang of guilt. *She* had never considered it before, either. What was wrong with her? No wonder her son didn't know how to be a child! She put the car in gear and headed toward the fast-food place with the playground.

They couldn't go very fast in town, of course, especially with all the stop signs and lights between the church and the Bypass. Nevertheless, the wind felt wonderful on her face and in her hair. The others seemed to enjoy it, too, judging by their laughter and smiles. She made a right hand turn onto the highway 81 bypass, and the pace slowed further. The whole county seemed to have come into town that day.

Bolton shook his head. "Traffic's as bad here as in a big city, don't you think?"

Clarice shrugged and glanced into her rearview mirror. "I wouldn't know, frankly. The last time I was in a big city was, oh, six or seven years ago. It was the first time we'd left Trenton overnight. His father had business in Tulsa, and I went with him. My mother-in-law was alive then, and she looked after Trent. He was still in diapers." She saw from the corner of her eye that Bolton gave her a speculative look, but he said nothing, and she couldn't imagine what he was thinking. She dismissed the matter and concentrated on her driving.

Eventually they reached the fast-food place Bolton had suggested. Clarice parked the car and turned the mirror down to see what damage the wind had done to her hair. "You two go on in," she said. "I'll be along in a minute." But nobody moved. She stopped combing her fingers through her hair and looked around. Bolton was looking at her, and Trenton was looking at Bolton. She couldn't read either expression. "What?" she asked, her gaze working back and forth between them.

Bolton lifted a shoulder. "Nothing. We just prefer to wait. It can't take long. You already look great."

Her mouth fell open. He thought she looked great? The very idea did queer things to her stomach, and she shifted a nervous look over her shoulder at her son. Trenton was looking at his lap, a knowing little smile twisting his lips. She didn't even want to *think* about the implications of that. What she wanted to do, in fact, was run. She slapped the mirror back into place and fumbled for the door handle. "Uh, I—I'm ready!"

She hopped out of the car and practically ran for the restaurant, the heels of her oh-so-sensible pumps clacking on the pavement. Bolton and Trenton caught up with and passed her. When she got there, Bolton was holding the door open for her and Trenton's face was solemn to the point of silliness. She marched past them and breezed into the restaurant, her cheeks burning red. She wanted to slap people, push them out of her way. What was wrong with her?

She got in line at the registers and composed herself, pulling deep, silent breaths to still the wild thumping of her heart. His was not the first compliment she'd ever received, for pity's sake. Besides, he hadn't really meant anything by it. He'd just wanted to hurry her because he was a gentleman and didn't want to leave her alone in the car. And Trenton? He was confused. Yes, that was it. Trenton was confused and... *She* was the one confused. *That* was the whole problem, and what a pathetic statement it was about the condition of her mind, not to mention her nonexistent love life. Good grief, she was having fantasies about a minister!

When the minister eased into line behind her and laid a companionable hand on her shoulder, she nearly jumped

out of her skin. "Hey, hold on there," he said quietly.
"Nobody's going to bite you."

"I—I know that! You just startled me."

"I wanted to tell you that lunch is on me."

"Oh, no, I couldn't—"

"I insist."

"No, really—"

His hands clamped down on her shoulders. "Clarice," he
said silkily into her ear, "shut up and go find us a table."

He left no doubt that he meant business, and she was only
too glad to get away. She started off swiftly, but he reached
out and grabbed her hand, turning her back.

"I forgot to ask what you want to eat."

She pulled her hand free, flipping it through the air. "A,
oh..." She looked helplessly at the menu, without really
seeing anything, and said, "Salad! Salad will do nicely.
And, ah, tea, ice tea." She exhaled with relief, turned and
got the heck out of there. She didn't see the troubled look
that followed her or the speculative one her son directed up
at Bolton Charles.

By the time they came with the food trays, Clarice had
once more talked herself into a calm state of mind. And
once more it vanished the moment Bolton smiled at her.
Seemingly oblivious to the panic he incited in her, he placed
her tea and salad in front of her, laid down a napkin and a
fork and slid into the seat next to Trent. They divided up the
remainder of food and drinks on the tray. Clarice watched,
feeling ridiculous and neglectful as Bolton tucked a napkin
into her son's lap. Trenton dug in with obvious relish, and
to her consternation Bolton leaned forward.

"Something wrong with your salad?"

"What? Oh. No, nothing." She picked up her fork and
poked at the shredded lettuce.

"Trent said you didn't care for salad dressing, but maybe you'd like some extra lemon or something."

"Lemon?"

He captured her gaze with his and held it. "Some people prefer to eat their salads with lemon juice as opposed to eating it dry," he said as if speaking to a child. "Would you like me to get you some lemon?"

She shook her head, dropped her eyes to her lunch, and managed to say, "No, thank you."

After that, she concentrated on eating, forking the lettuce and occasional sliver of carrot into her mouth, chewing, and swallowing. The single wedge of tomato required special concentration as she ground it into pulpy pieces with the side of her fork and intently chewed each one. Just as she'd worked her way through her own small lunch, Trenton announced that he was ready to go out to the playground. Bolton got up and let him out of the booth, then sat back down again. Clarice lurched to her feet, intent on escaping with her son, but Bolton's hand shot out and prevented her.

"He'll be all right," he said gently. "Sit down. I want to talk to you."

She looked longingly after her son. "The sign says they're supposed to have adult supervision."

He glanced over his shoulder. "There are plenty of adults out there. Sit down."

Deprived of her excuse, she slowly sank back onto the bench seat. Bolton popped a few fries into his mouth, chewed and swallowed. "I've been wanting to ask why I haven't ever seen you at church. Do you attend elsewhere?"

Church. She almost slumped with relief. Church was certainly a nice, safe subject to discuss with a minister. She made herself smile. "No, we don't attend elsewhere. It's

Wallis. He doesn't like to go out now that he's confined to the wheelchair, so we sort of hold our own service on Sunday mornings. Wallis chooses a passage from the Bible, and I read it aloud and answer any questions Trenton may have about it."

"He has quite a few questions, does he?"

"More and more as he gets older."

"Don't you think he might benefit from an organized Bible study, then?"

"Yes, I'm sure he would."

"Good. Now what about you?"

She blinked at him. "Me?"

He laid his hands flat against the tabletop. They were large hands with wide palms and long, gracefully tapered fingers with healthy, oval nails. "We have a Bible class at the church for women your age. It's a friendly bunch. I'm sure you'd like them."

"I—I'm sure I would."

"You wouldn't have to stop Wallis's private services," he pointed out. "You could always do both."

"I don't know. I'll have to speak to Wallis."

He arched an eyebrow. "Oh, really? I was under the impression that you were taking charge of your own life."

"I am."

"So what's the problem?"

"There's no problem, and I don't want to cause any."

He looked down, pressed his napkin to his mouth and wadded it up. "If you don't want to come, just say so."

"It's not that!"

He pinned her with dark, intense eyes. "Then what is it?"

She couldn't even breathe, let alone formulate a coherent answer. She just sat there with her mouth open, like a fish out of water. To her utter confusion, he smiled and changed the subject.

"I like your hair. You got a good cut. Mine always take two or three weeks to look like it's supposed to."

"Maybe you need to change barbers," she managed to mumble, flattered but shaken that he'd even noticed.

He laughed. "And insult a faithful member of my congregation?"

She grimaced. "That is awkward."

He shrugged. "Comes with the territory. There are worse things than a bad haircut."

She didn't know what to say to that, so she didn't say anything at all. Instead, she watched Trenton out the window. He was crawling across a rope bridge strung between two barrels suspended no more than three feet off the ground. Two other boys were running around with toy guns pretending to shoot each other. Trenton stopped to watch them, and they shot right through him, ignoring him as if he wasn't there. Even at a distance, she could not miss the longing look in her son's eyes. She bit her lip. Oh, why had she let this happen? She wanted to cry. Bolton noticed and looked over his shoulder. He sized up the situation in a moment, and when he turned back to her, he reached for her hand.

"He's going to be all right," he said, turning her hand over in his. "He's a great kid, Clarice. A super kid. Bright, sensitive, caring. He just needs a little practice with kids his own age. That's another reason I want to see you get him involved in Little League, and it wouldn't hurt if he attended Bible study on Sunday mornings, either. I'll pave the way for him, if you'll let me."

The last was as much a question as a statement. She made an instant decision, telling herself that it had nothing to do with the way that heat was spreading up her arm. "Yes, please."

He smiled and gripped her hand tighter. "I'll call his Sunday school teacher and tell her to expect him. She'll introduce him to the other kids and make sure he gets involved in a group activity. I'll also see what I can find out about Little League sports in this area. It may be too late to get him on a baseball team for this season, and it's definitely too early for football, but there is bound to be *something* gearing up. What about swimming lessons? Has Trent been taught to swim?"

She nodded. "I insisted. We have a pool."

"Let me guess. Private lessons."

She winced. "How did you know?"

"Would Wallis Revere send his only grandson down to the public pool?"

"No, but I should have insisted he do so." She sighed and dropped her gaze, carefully extracting her hand from his. That was when she saw the bruise. "Bolton!" He attempted to close his hand, but she grabbed his wrist and pried his fingers down. The center of his palm—his left palm, not the right, which was the one he'd shown Trenton—was a purplish red.

"You're hurt!"

"It's just a bruise."

"Your hand could be broken! Of all the idiotic—"

"It's not broken," he said, suddenly gripping her fingers to make his point. "See? It doesn't even hurt. And I don't want Trent thinking it's his fault. That wasn't the first time I've pulled that particularly stupid stunt. I knew better, and I did it anyway, but if he sees or hears of this bruise he'll blame himself, so not another word, you hear me?"

She nodded, so profoundly sorry and yet grateful at the same time that tears gathered in her eyes. Bolton laughed and gently smoothed his thumbs over her cheekbones.

"Well, now I know who he gets the guilts from," he said teasingly, then he added in a soft voice, "as well as his good looks."

Her mouth fell open again. He shook his head and chucked her under the chin. She snapped it shut just as Trenton ran up to the table. Bolton made the transition as smoothly as buttering bread. "Ready to go?" he asked the boy.

Trent nodded, and Bolton piled their refuse on the tray. Trent went to dump it in the trash can, and Bolton turned to follow, but Clarice grabbed his arm before he could get away.

"Thank you," she said, "for lunch and..." She couldn't think how to finish the sentence without embarrassing herself.

He smiled and waved her in front of him. "You're welcome." With that, he ushered her out after her son.

Chapter Three

"What's the matter, pal? Want to talk about it?"

Trent hunched one shoulder in reply, then shook his head. "Nothing."

Like mother, like son, Bolton thought, gazing up through the dark green tree leaves overhead. He wondered if she knew just how much like her Trenton was. He smoothed his hand over the boy's nape and waited. Finally Trent looked up.

"Did you know my dad?"

Bolton leaned forward on the hard bench, elbows on knees. "No. Why do you ask?" He got that shrug again.

"I just wondered. I thought maybe if you knew him, then that's how you'd know what I like and...maybe that's why I like you so much. I mean, maybe I remembered you from before, only I don't *know* it. Kinda stupid, huh?"

"It's not stupid at all," Bolton told him. "Good friends, even if they're new friends, often feel as if they've known each other all their lives."

"But what makes it that way?"

Bolton clasped his hands together. "I'm not sure I know. Maybe it's what they have in common."

Trenton screwed up his face. "What's that mean?"

Bolton sighed inwardly. He wasn't doing a very good job at this. He spread his hands and tried again. "Well, let's take us for instance. We both like sports, so that's something we have in common."

Trent's face lit up. "Oh! And hamburgers and fries."

"What?"

"We both like burgers and fries!" he said excitedly.

Bolton grinned. "Right. That's something else we have in common."

"And chocolate milk shakes!" Trent went on excitedly. "And driving with the top down, and blue! Our favorite color is blue! Oh, and General! Don't forget General."

Bolton laughed from sheer pleasure. "Now how could I forget that scraggly old tomcat? You know what else? There's that red wagon you've got, too."

"Yeah! You had one when you were a boy!"

"I sure did. But it's even more than all that, Trent. You and I, we *think* alike, even *feel* alike in lots of ways."

Now the boy seemed genuinely intrigued. "What do you mean?"

"Well, I've noticed a few things about you that remind me of myself when I was your age. For example, you're a little shy around new people. You don't always know what to say or do to make them like you. You haven't learned yet that the thing to do is just to be yourself. I was exactly the same way when I was eight."

"You were?" Trent's eyes were big and round, and his voice was imbued with awe.

Bolton chuckled. "Yes, I was, and the next time you feel like swallowing your tongue, I want you to remember it."

Trent's mouth was hanging open. "That's just how it is! You're so afraid you're gonna say something dumb, you practically choke!"

"It gets better," Bolton promised him, "and the more you just try to be yourself, the quicker it happens. Remember that, okay?"

The boy nodded solemnly. "I'll remember."

Bolton clapped his shoulder affectionately, then glanced at his watch. "Mmm, time we headed back, I guess."

They got up and ambled across the grass toward the car. Bolton noticed wryly that when he hooked his thumbs in his hip pockets, Trent did the same. He wondered if the other people in the park would assume they were father and son. Trent craned his head back to look up at him.

"Hey, Bolt?"

"Hmm?" That nickname still made him want to snicker, but he did his best not to let Trent know that.

"Do you think you would've liked my dad?"

What a question. Would he have liked Wallis Revere's only son, the son Wallis had been determined to mold into a likeness of himself? He cleared his throat. "I would have if he was anything like you."

"That's what I thought," Trent said. "Grandpa says I am like him."

"Oh?" Somehow Bolton had his doubts, but he kept them to himself.

"Yeah," Trent went on, "and you'd have other things in collman."

"Common," Bolton corrected lightly.

"Common," Trent repeated. "Like my mom."

Bolton stopped and looked down at the boy. "I'm not sure I follow that."

Trent narrowed his eyes. "Well, you like her, don't you?"

Bolton considered an evasion, then thought better of it. "Yes," he finally said, "very much."

"Well, he liked her, too, didn't he? I mean, they got married and all."

"I see your point," Bolton muttered, starting the trek toward the car again. He had a feeling he knew what was coming next, and he wasn't wrong.

"Do you like her that much?"

He took it in stride. "Enough to marry her, you mean?"

"Yes."

"I don't know, Trent. I haven't had much opportunity to find out. In case you haven't noticed, she's avoiding me."

"Yeah. Why is she?"

"I don't know, pal. Maybe she just doesn't like me as much as I like her."

"Aw, that's not it," Trent insisted. "You know what it is? I think you just make her shy."

Bolton smiled. "You could be right about that. What do you think I ought to do about it?"

"I don't know. Whatever my father did, I guess."

Bolton let his hand fall upon the boy's shoulder. "Now that, my friend, is good advice."

They walked on in silence for a few moments, then Trent asked, "Do you say good advice, Bolt?"

"Sometimes I do."

"Well, that's something else we got in common, huh?"

Bolton laughed and put his hand in his pocket for his keys. "And that's not the end of it, I'm sure."

Trent nodded, serious as a judge. "That's what I figure, too."

Bolton wanted to hug him, but he didn't dare. Instead, he unlocked the car door and opened it for him. Trent scrambled in and went to work on the seat belt. He liked to do it for himself even though it was a particularly difficult restraint system, so Bolton resisted the urge to help him. He had the car started before the belt was secured, but at last the buckle clicked into place, and Bolton put the car in gear.

Trent was quiet on the ride across town, and he'd given Bolton plenty to think about, so conversation was kept to a minimum. Bolton could feel the boy worrying something around in his head, though, so he wasn't surprised when, just as they turned into the Revere estate drive, he piped up again.

"Bolt," he said gravely, "I don't remember my dad."

Apparently it was some kind of momentous confession, so Bolton considered carefully before he replied. He brought the car around in front of the house and parked, then turned to face the boy. "I know what you mean, Trent. Forgetting is a pretty normal reaction to death. My wife died a couple of years ago, and sometimes I get sort of sad because I can't remember some little thing about her, like what size shoe she wore or if she liked a certain movie."

"Yeah, but I don't remember my dad *at all*," Trent said, "and Grandpa keeps saying how I shouldn't ever forget him. It makes me feel bad."

"Well, you shouldn't feel bad, Trent. You were only— what?—three when he died? No one could reasonably expect you to remember him. What your grandfather really wants is for you to remember who your father was and that he loved you and that he would love you today, too, if he could."

"You really think so?"

"I do."

The boy seemed to digest that, but those eyes were just slits and his bottom lip was well chewed when he looked up again. "You think my dad would mind that I like you so much?" he asked softly.

They had arrived, at last, at the very heart of the problem. Bolton put his hand on the boy's shoulder. "Maybe, if he was here. Dads like to be their sons' best friends, you know. On the other hand, I think that if he'd have known he wasn't going to be here with you, he'd have wanted you to have a friend like me. I know this for certain, Trent. You shouldn't feel disloyal to your father's memory just because you like me." *And neither should your mother,* he added mentally.

Trenton nodded his understanding, and those green, green eyes were wide open now. A movement at the edge of his vision caught Bolton's attention, and he turned his head in that direction. The door was open, and Clarice stood framed in it.

"Time to go in," he said.

They got out of the car and walked side by side to the door.

"I thought I heard someone out here," Clarice said brightly. She bent to drop a kiss on the top of her son's head. "Have a good time?"

"Sure."

"Great. Well, thank you, Bolton. We don't want to keep you."

He ignored that obvious invitation to leave and rubbed a circle on Trent's back. "Why don't you go on in now, pal? I want to talk to your mom."

"Okay. See ya', Bolt."

"Friday, three-thirty," Bolton confirmed.

With a nod, Trent went inside and closed the door. That was one smart kid. Bolton put a foot up on the doorstep and looked down at Clarice. She was drawn up tight as a bow string. He smiled.

"Your son and I had an interesting conversation today."

"Oh?"

"Mmm-hmm. Among other things, we talked about his father."

That had her slack-jawed. "You're kidding! Trenton never talks about his father."

"He did today."

"But why with you? Why not with me?"

Bolton pursed his lips. "Maybe he sensed I wouldn't be upset by his choice of topic."

"And I would," she said bitterly, taking the thought to its logical conclusion. "I have made so many mistakes with that child."

Bolton shook his head. "Could've fooled me. That's a great kid, in case you haven't noticed, and great kids don't just happen."

She smiled up at him. Her moss-green eyes sparked with warm, yellow gold. "That's a very kind thing to say."

"That's the truth," he told her, "but if you think I'm so kind, maybe you'll answer a question for me."

"If I can."

He scratched behind his ear, trying to think how best to put it. Well, there was only one way really. "Look," he said, "you won't come along with Trent and me. You won't come to church. You won't even stop and chat a while unless I make a federal case out of it. So what I want to know is, how did your husband do it? Get you to loosen up, I mean, *before* he was your husband."

The look on her face was incredulous. He took exception to it.

"Don't look at me like that. I'm only following some good advice."

"Trent?" she queried, nearly choking on it.

"Out of the mouths of babes, as they say. So how did he do it? I'm serious about this. I really want to know."

"Well, he... he..." She fluttered her hands helplessly. "I don't know! He just kept at it. He was very persistent. The Reveres can be very persistent."

Bolton smiled. "Ah."

"Besides," she went on, "I was at a very vulnerable point. Right after I graduated high school, my parents were killed in a car wreck. I didn't have anyplace to go, anyone to go to."

"I'm sorry," he said gently. "But that certainly explains a lot."

"Such as?"

"Such as how a sweet woman like you wound up married to the heir apparent of the likes of Wallis Revere."

She gazed up at him with implacable but oddly vulnerable eyes. "You shouldn't say such things."

"Why not?"

"You don't really know me. You didn't know him."

"I want to know you. As for him, I expect he was a good deal like Wallis, wasn't he?"

Her jaw worked forward and back. "In many ways."

"I thought as much."

She ignored the comment. "Did my son really tell you to ask me that?"

He chuckled. "Not exactly. We talked about common interests, how they make a basis for a friendship, and he figured that because he and I have a lot in common, his father and I would have, too. The one thing he knew for sure we would have had in common, though, was you."

"Me?" she squeaked.

"It makes perfect sense. The man had to like you—he married you, right?"

She did not reply to that, merely folded her arms. "Go on."

"Well, it's obvious that *I* like you. Even an eight-year-old picked up on it. And it's also obvious that you've been avoiding me like the plague. Trent said it's because I make you shy, and when I asked him what he thought I ought to do about it, he said he supposed I should do whatever his father did. So that's why I want to know. See? Perfect sense."

She glared at him, and her hands fell to her hips. "That's the most nonsensical thing I've ever heard!"

"No, it isn't," he said reasonably. "You're just ticked off because you told me before you understood why I wanted to know."

"I'm ticked off because you've been discussing very personal, even intimate, details of my life with my son!"

He was shaking his head before she even finished. "Wrong again. Trent doesn't know the intimate details of your life. If he did, I wouldn't have had to ask, now would I?"

"That's not the point!"

"True enough. The point is, you like me almost as much as I like you, and that makes you very, very nervous, doesn't it?"

"No such thing!" she huffed.

He clucked his tongue. "Must be tough. Here you are just about to finally get your life together, and up turns a piece that doesn't fit. A tall, cheeky preacher who insists on seeing you as a whole woman instead of just a mother. Well, that piece is going to keep on turning up, lady, until you find a place to put it, even if it's the last piece to the puzzle. Count on it."

"You were asked to take a hand with my son," she reminded him tartly, "not me!"

"Those are the breaks, Clarice," he retorted. "We often get more than we ask for, and when we do, we just have to deal with it."

"That's a very self-serving opinion!"

"That's a fact."

"The facts according to Bolton Charles!" she snapped. "Do you deliver them from the pulpit the same way?"

He gritted his teeth through a smile. "I think I'll go while I still have a grip on my temper." He turned and started down the walk. "So long, Clarice. I'm going now." At the last moment he tossed over his shoulder, "But I'll be back."

She whirled, slamming her way through the door. He shivered at the sound. Ah, well, if persistence truly was the key, that door would open to him again. And if it wasn't? He wondered if God was trying to take him down a peg. If so, his ego was going to come out of this bruised and bloody. But not broken. Never broken. He knew his God well enough to know that, and he knew, too, that the risk was worth it. After all, he only had pride to lose—and much to win.

Clarice put her back to the door and fumed. No one had ever made her as angry as that man! What had happened to the nice preacher she'd called on at the church that first day? A little voice in the back of her mind commented that he'd turned into a *man,* an *attractive* man, and she did not have room in her life just now for a man of any sort, but certainly not a minister.

No option existed for them. Why couldn't he see that? One simply did not indulge in any sort of flirtation with a minister, and an affair was out of the question, for her as much as for him. She knew herself well enough to know that she would find no joy in an illicit liaison. But marriage, too, was not open for consideration, *especially* marriage to a

minister. The last thing she needed was another man to run
her life for her, so why on earth would she even entertain the
notion of marrying a man whose career subjected her to the
strictures and judgments of the church and the community? The very idea was insane.

All she wanted was a measure of control over her own
hours and days. She wanted to be a good parent. She wanted
to give her son options for his own life. It meant walking a
fine line, and she'd walked fine lines of one sort or another
all her life. She could do it now, provided she could just find
the correct line to walk. It was harder than it might seem to
an outsider.

She had no actual means of support. Wallis Revere hadn't
yielded a single string of his financial empire to his son.
They had lived by Wallis's generosity before Trent Sr.'s
death, and they lived by Wallis's generosity now. More-
over, she had never done a day's work for pay in her life,
and even if she had possessed some talent that made her fit
for employment, the local economy had little to offer a single mother. The decline in the oil business had thrown a
large segment of the community out of work. There were
men with whole families to support taking any minimum
wage job they could find. Any way she looked at it, she was
dependent on Wallis, so it was within the framework of Revere House that she had to work for her measure of independence. To do otherwise would have been folly of the
worst sort for the most important person in her life, her son.

It was possible that Bolton Charles did not know what he
asked of her with his smiles and looks and provocative talk,
but she vetoed the possibility of explaining it to him. His
intent was fixed now. Talk of any sort would only serve to
encourage him, so she would just have to keep her distance. The otherwise kindly minister was no Revere. He
would give up and fix his interest elsewhere.

She couldn't help wondering, though, why she seemed to intrigue him. Was it possible that she shared similarities with his late wife? Or was Bolton Charles one of those men who thought it his duty to rescue every widow woman he found from her fate? She didn't suppose she would ever know, but she couldn't help wondering.

Friday afternoon, Bolton paused on the doorstep of Revere House, Trenton by his side, and gave off his most charming smile. "Care to join us for a tall, cold ice pop, Clarice?"

"No, thank you."

"Nothing sweet and cool for you on a hot summer day, hmm?"

"Nothing tall and tart, either."

"Ouch."

"Have a good time," she said complacently to her son, then she stepped back and closed the door in his face. Round one for her. Well, it was a start.

Sunday morning, Bolton stood on the sidewalk in front of the church, shaking hands and keeping a watchful eye on the cars dropping off youngsters for Bible study. When the white convertible pulled up to the curb, he excused himself and stepped over to open the door. Trent squeezed out from behind his mother's seat, squashing her into the steering wheel in the process. Bolton smiled down at him, gave his head a pat and straightened his tie.

"You know where to go, pal. Don't want to be late."

With a wave to his mom, Trent took off. Bolton had not yet relinquished his hold on the car door, and instead of closing it, he pushed it wider and bent down so he could direct his smile point-blank at his target.

"I'm expected back at the house, Bolton," she said dryly.

"Not staying for Bible study yourself, then?"

"I'm expected back at the house."

"You can stand up to that old man anytime you want to, you know."

She cocked her head to one side and fixed a sweet smile in place. "Figured that out, have you?"

He clapped a hand over his heart. "Score another one for the lady. But the game's a long way from over."

"This isn't a game, Bolton. This is my life."

"Good, because I want in your life, Clarice. Just give me a chance. You may find out you need me."

"The only thing I need right now, Bolton, is a cup of coffee," she said with false politeness. She put the car in gear and let it roll forward a few feet, then closed the door and drove away. When Bolton brought Trenton home after services, she would be out.

Tuesday evening Bolton set up a play period with the grandchildren of his secretary, Cora Beemis. The kids were younger than Trenton, so Bolton had wisely put the thing to him as a baby-sitting venture. As a result, Trenton considered himself employed. Clarice thought Bolton should be apprised, so at the door she attempted to slip him a five dollar bill with which to "pay" Trenton. He pushed it back into her hand and folded her fingers around it.

"We've already agreed that payment will come in the form of a banana split."

She had to hand it to him—he was on top of things. But somebody had to pay for the treat, and she knew darned well that Bolton was not turning in expense reports to Wallis. "Let me buy the banana splits," she urged.

He shot her a grin. "Fine by me. But not tonight. Cora's left the makings at her house. You can buy me a banana split any other time your little heart desires, though. How about Friday?''

''How about I give you the five bucks and you can treat yourself anytime you want?''

''What's so wrong with going out for ice cream with me?''

''There's nothing wrong with it, Bolton, but there's nothing *right* with it, either.''

''I beg to differ.''

''Begging doesn't become you, Bolton.''

''Even sarcasm becomes you, Clarice.''

''Touché. And good night.''

As he and Trent turned from the door, Bolton sighed. ''I don't think I make your mom shy anymore, pal.''

''Nope, but you sure make her mad.''

Bolton stopped and grinned down at his small companion. ''Is that right?''

Trent screwed up his eyes and chomped down on his lip, nodding. ''She says I wouldn't understand, but I think I might.''

Bolton chuckled. ''No sale, pal. I've already had my ears pinned for discussing your mother with you once, and I never make the same mistake twice.''

Trent shook his head in disgust and headed on down the walk. ''Women!'' he snorted in that men's club voice he'd adopted of late.

Bolton smiled, but it faded, and he sighed again. ''No, just, 'Woman!''' he said softly. ''That one, particular, stubborn woman.''

But he wasn't ready to give up yet. Patience, he reminded himself, was a virtue.

Some ninety minutes later, he reminded himself that patience was not only a virtue but often a necessity. Since the moment that he'd arrived at the home of Cora Beemis, her four-year-old granddaughter Mellie had been parked in his lap, her elbow in his ribs, her thumb in her mouth, the heels of her shoes dug in against the tops of his knees. Nothing he tried would dislodge her. Even the suggestion that she run off and play with the boys produced a dangerous wobble in her chin and a threatening sparkle in her eyes. ''I wan' pway wif you,'' she would say around her thumb.

Bolton resorted to wrapping his arms around her upper body just beneath her arms and hauling her along with him when he went to see what latest catastrophe her brother Cory's bloodcurdling whoops heralded. She accepted this indignity good-naturedly, her body as limp as a rag doll's. He had never dreamed that four-year-olds could be so heavy or six-year-olds so destructive. Cory seemed to believe it was his duty to reduce his grandmother's residence to a shambles.

The kid attacked the television in Cora's den with a bow and rubber-tipped arrows, one of which a big-eyed Trent accidentally took in the cheek. After Bolton confiscated the weapons, Cory very ingeniously made himself into a human bowling ball, designated Trent as the pin, and rolled himself down the hall fast enough to knock down Trent and rattle the china cabinet in the dining room upon his collision with an adjoining wall. Mellie dangling over his forearm, Bolton laid down the law: No more bowling. Undaunted and with no apparent resentment, Cory fashioned an airplane from an arrangement of kitchen chairs and a cardboard box. He very generously assigned Trent the position of pilot and took the copilot's chair for himself, then abruptly transformed himself into a hijacker, extorted a trillion dollars in ransom and parachuted out into the wilderness next to the kitchen table, threatening the continuity of the bay window in the breakfast nook. Trent very conscientiously tried to prevent the bailout by shooting him, but his finger was either unloaded or he simply missed, as Cory insisted.

Bolton considered tying the little hellion to a chair in the living room, but a short whispered conversation with Trent gave him a truly brilliant idea and won him an inventive and willing coconspirator. With some practiced urging from him, the champion of his weight class agreed to give lucky Cory some very interesting lessons in competitive wrestling. With Mellie hanging about his neck, Bolton moved the coffee table to one side and drew a ring with a spoon drawn against the nap through the living room carpet. Trent and Cory removed their shoes, and Trent began a long, involved lecture with enough grappling holds thrown in to sustain Cory's interest. Then the real demonstrations began.

Trent's expertise was remarkable to Bolton, but the maturity and control he displayed in keeping Cory occupied and confined without exhausting the younger boy's interest was nothing short of amazing. Bolton felt unabashed, if unwarranted, pride in the way Trent handled himself. He knew, of course, that he had contributed nothing at all to Trent's development to date, but he could not help feeling that no other boy could possibly display such strength of character, such wisdom, such judgment, and he thanked God that he'd been tapped to provide "influence" to Wallis Revere's grandson rather than to Cora Beemis's!

Giving credit where credit was due, however, he had to admit that Cory was not only a good sport but doggedly and cheerfully determined. No matter how many times Trent pinned him, and they were considerable, the boy kept coming back for more, so that by the time Cora Beemis and her daughter, Lissa Earlie, returned from their night out, both Cory and Trent were exhausted from their efforts. Bolton himself felt as though he'd been put through a pepper mill and ground to a fine pulp. Even Cora, scatterbrained as she was, realized that "Bolt" had had his hands full and that it would be best to rescue him from the adoring clutches of her granddaughter as quickly as possible.

Unfortunately, Mellie was not through "pwaying wif the wevewend" and had to be coaxed away from him with the promised banana split. Trent proved too sleepy-eyed to eat much of his, but Cory, despite his own exhaustion, ignored his mother's admonitions and ate enough to make himself sick. Without too much confusion, Bolton managed to make a fairly quick exit, which allowed Trent to maintain his dignity by walking out to the car on his own two legs, but by the time they reached Revere House, he was snoring softly, his head against the window.

Bolton didn't have the heart to wake the boy, so he carried him to the house, cradled against his shoulder, and leaned on the doorbell. Clarice opened the door, her face troubled, and he knew she'd probably looked first through the peephole.

"He's all right," Bolton told her quietly, "just played out, but I don't think you can carry him to his room. So if you'll just show me the way..."

Her face solemn, Clarice nodded and stepped back to allow him through the door. After closing it behind him, she hurried ahead and led the way across the entry, up the stairs and along the landing to a room at the far end. It was not, as Bolton had supposed, the boy's bedroom but a kind of den. A television set flickered in near silence in the softly lit room. Clarice switched it off as she led him past it to one of a pair of doors set in opposite corners of the room. It was there that Bolton found the small bed upon which he could finally lay the boy. He knew that his part in putting the boy to bed was done, but he imagined that Clarice, small and delicate as she was, would have a time of it undressing her son alone, so he set to work doing so himself, quickly slipping off shoes and socks, jeans and shirt, leaving the child clad only in his undershorts. Clarice pulled the covers up over him and lovingly smoothed the hair back from his forehead.

Trent rolled over and yawned without opening his eyes, muttering, "G'night, Mom." Then very sleepily, he added, "G'night, Bolt."

Something warm and soft seemed to expand inside Bolton's chest. He whispered good night, but could not seem to turn away from the little form cuddled beneath the covers, the tawny head pillowed upon folded hands. *Such a fine boy,* he was thinking when he felt a hand upon his arm. He turned slightly and caught at it as it fell away. She dropped her gaze, and even in the dim light from the doorway, he could see that her face paled. He felt a flare of anger and a sudden determination to bring this thing between them to a head. Grasping her hand tightly, he pulled her from the room, and there beyond the closed door of her son's room, he used his free hand to force her gaze up to meet his.

"What is it about me you find so distasteful?" he demanded in a rough whisper.

Her green eyes registered shock. "Why, nothing!"

Nothing? That good news swept through him in a happy rush, and without thought or design or even comprehension, he did what seemed the most natural thing in the world. He took her in his arms and kissed her.

Chapter Four

She went from one shock to another, from the craziness of hearing that anything might be considered distasteful about Bolton Charles to the wildness of being held and kissed by the most attractive man she had met since...well, by the most attractive man she had met. It was quite a unique experience, and her mind seemed to have divided its functions. While one part cataloged the sensations that rushed through her as his arms came around her and his mouth descended to meet hers, another was busily comparing every aspect of this event with similar ones in her past. She found, to her surprise, that the number was very few, and she somehow remained aware of every nuance of this very present occurrence while calling to mind those few other instances.

It was utterly amazing, the feel of long, strong arms folded tightly about her, the commanding possessiveness of a wide, mobile, finely drawn mouth, the overwhelming breadth of a hard, subtly molded chest that tapered to a narrow waist around which her own arms seemed to find a very natural fit. And heat. She felt such heat. It surrounded her, radiated from every point of contact, filled her, flashed within the depths of her body, melted her bones. She felt it most keenly in her mouth, moist, velvety heat tasting faintly of a rich, familiar sweetness, but she felt it heavily, too, between her shoulder blades where his hand splayed, along the length of her thighs where they met his and deep within the pit of her belly where an unfamiliar flame burned.

That other part of her mind relived in a flash of memory a day when Trenton's father had maneuvered her around the corner of a building and pressed her against the brick as he'd kissed her. She had been shocked that day and scared they were going to be caught—and all of seventeen. Over the following years, he had kissed her unexpectedly at other times, when he was pleased about something else and wanted to share it with her, when she had worried aloud and he'd wanted to distract her, and once when he'd wanted to impress his friends. Had he ever kissed her like this just because he'd wanted to?

She pushed that thought away. It was unfair. Her husband had been dead five long years now. And she didn't want another, especially not a minister. The thought occurred to her that, such being the case, she ought to disengage, and yet she held on, blending her mouth with his, exulting in the awareness of his potent maleness and her own powerful femininity. In the end, he was the one to break the kiss, to pull his mouth reluctantly from hers and press her head into the hollow of his shoulder, his arms tightening about her. Oddly, she found this unacceptable. That kiss had been desire—sudden, sharp, overwhelming. She had felt it, wallowed in it, but this... This was *affection,* deep, abiding affection, and it terrified her, struck bluntly at the very foundation of her independence. Desire she could revel in, flirt with and refuse. Affection would be much harder to reject. After all, no one would condemn a woman for protecting her virtue, but a woman who insisted upon protecting her heart could well be viewed as selfish and mean. She did not want to be seen as selfish or mean, but she *would* not be seen as weak. She pushed herself away.

Bolton looked down, his features softened by a wealth of rich emotion, emotion he had no right whatsoever to feel. Clarice lifted her chin.

"How dare you?"

His brows went up, then slowly down again. After a long moment of silence, he spoke in a quiet, husky voice. "Forgive me, I . . . presumed too much, obviously."

"You have from the beginning," she told him, wincing inwardly at the sharpness of her tone.

His mouth crooked up on one side. "So it seems. It isn't like me, though. I've always been a good reader of other people."

She blanched, guilt swamping her. She fought it off, her jaw setting. "So what if I like you?" she demanded. "Since when does that have to mean that I want to be involved with you?"

He stiffened. "You're quite right, of course. As I said, I presumed too much. It won't happen again."

That was exactly what she wanted to hear. Why, then, did it deflate her so? She drew herself up, strengthening her resolve as she stiffened her spine. "I'm glad you finally understand," she said calmly. "You . . . you're a nice man, Bolton. I'd like to consider you a friend. God knows I'm grateful to you for what you're doing . . . have done for my son, but . . ."

"But friendship is all you want from me," he finished for her.

She nodded, feeling both gratitude and an odd, almost formless disappointment. "I didn't mean to let you think otherwise."

"You didn't. All right, if friendship is what you want, friendship is what you'll get."

"Thank you." He really was a sweet man. "Like my son, I could use a good friend."

A look of *something* moved over his face. "Then you mean for me to continue with Trent?"

"Yes, of course—unless you'd rather not."

"No! I'm crazy about that kid. He's the best company I've had in a long time."

She smiled, suffused with pride. "I'm glad. He loves being with you, and he loves playing baseball."

He returned her smile. "First game Thursday night."

"I know. I'll be there."

"So will I."

"Good. I think it will help him to have you there."

"Oh, he'll do fine," Bolton assured her. "I had a word with his coach, you know—he's an old friend of mine. He says Trent's got more raw talent than any kid he's ever worked with."

"It was so good of you to get him onto a team after he'd missed the summer league tryouts," she said.

Bolton shrugged. "Wasn't anything I did. There was a vacancy on the team. They were rather desperate, in fact, for a good shortstop. Trent's good. That's why they took him even though he's younger than the other players. I tell you, if he'd been at tryouts, those coaches would've been fighting over him. He's something, that kid."

Clarice's heart flipped over in her chest. Did he know how much like a doting father he sounded? It struck her suddenly as unfair that they were asking him to play surrogate father to a boy who could never be his son. But they were

friends, weren't they, Bolton and Trenton? Shouldn't that
be enough? She wanted to ask but didn't dare. She couldn't
risk alerting Bolton to a problem which he might not have
thought of himself. He was so good for Trenton, and she
had to put her son's needs first. She banished any qualms.

"Well," she said, wanting him gone suddenly, "I guess
we'll see you Thursday evening."

He just looked at her for a moment, then ran a hand
down the back of his neck, nodding. "Right. Thursday." He
gave her a smile that was not reflected in eyes gone almost
bleak. "Good night. I'll, um, show myself out."

She folded her hands, fighting the impulse to turn away.
She would have to follow, of course, to lock the door, but
she needed some distance between herself and Bolton
Charles. He unnerved her, and somehow she always wound
up feeling guilty. She was so damned tired of feeling guilty!
She watched him leave the room and listened with relief to
his footsteps along the landing. The sounds gradually died
away, then some moments later she caught the faint *shoop*
of the door closing against the jamb. A hand fluttered up to
her forehead, but she forced it down. She had not believed
it would be easy. Taking charge of one's self was not easy,
let alone taking responsibility for a child, but she would do
it and continue doing it if it killed her. She knew her limitations, however, and because she did, Bolton Charles,
friend or no, would just have to look after himself. Somehow she thought he was up to it. She only hoped that she
was.

He was *so* nervous. She could see it in the slitted eyes, the
worried lip, the rigidly squared shoulders. Baseball, he had
explained, was different than wrestling. If he screwed up out
there on the field, the whole team suffered for it. Could she
say a prayer for him? He had intended to ask Bolton, but

Bolton *was* running late, and he didn't want to let down his teammates. Bolton was running late, and she couldn't help wondering if it had anything to do with her. Surely not. Would he punish her son because she had rebuffed his romantic advances? She couldn't believe it, but she had to wonder.

The umpire called the teams to play nearly a quarter hour late, and still Bolton had not arrived. Clarice smiled at the other parents around her as she craned her neck to search the perimeters of the area. The opposing team was called to bat, so Trent and his teammates took up positions on the field. The pitcher, who was one of the coaches, the customary fast-pitch overhanded throw having been judged detrimental to the development of growing arms and shoulders, walked up onto the mound and sized up the batter. He wound up and let go what seemed to Clarice a rather tepid offering, but to her surprise, the batter swung and the umpire called a first strike. The crowd was chattering, talking amongst themselves, yelling encouragement and advice to various players. She heard someone addressing her son.

"Heads up, shortstop! Heads up! He's gonna connect!"

She looked behind her, spying a corpulent fellow in tight stretch shorts and a faded football jersey. He dropped his gaze on her face, neither friendly nor hostile, then flicked his attention back to the field. At that moment, she heard a sharp crack, and the crowd erupted in screams. She whipped her head around in time to see Trenton lower his glove and pivot in a circle, his head following the arc of the ball. She felt a stab of panic. Why wasn't he going after it? Wasn't he supposed to catch it? He had explained the function of shortstop in explicit detail, but she hadn't actually been able to follow him. She clamped down on her bottom lip.

Oh, God, don't let him screw up. He'll be so disappointed!

The ball hit the ground and rolled. Another kid farther out picked it up and looked quickly from side to side before letting fly. Her heart jumped up in her throat. The ball was whizzing right toward Trenton. The batter was running from second base to third, his little legs pumping. Trenton stepped directly into his path and went into a crouch, glove up at chest height. The ball socked right into his glove. The runner tried to step around him, but Trenton lunged to the side and tagged him with the ball. The screaming around her intensified, then was instantly muted by applause. Clarice realized that she was on her feet. The fat guy behind her was yelling, "Atta boy! Atta boy! Good play! Good play!"

She whirled around and demanded, "What happened? Did he do well?"

His gaze was blank. "The shortstop?"

"Yes."

"He did great! He got the runner out."

"Oh. And that's good for our side?"

He looked at her like she was some alien life form. "Two more outs and we get to bat," he said in an incredulous tone, as if that explained everything.

Clarice turned around and sat down, unwilling to embarrass herself further. A chuckle in her ear sent her pivoting sideways. Bolton grinned at her.

"I told you he'd be okay."

"You're here!"

"Better late than never." His grin faded. "Sorry. It was an emergency."

"What happened?"

"One of our nursing-home residents has been transferred to the hospital. The family's upset, of course. Death would be a release in this case, but the death watch is always difficult. I promised I'd return later, and I may have to leave early if they page me." He indicated the beeper attached to his belt.

Clarice bit her lip, repentant for earlier suspicions. "I'm so sorry. You shouldn't have come."

"Nonsense. My uninterrupted presence will be required later but not now. Besides, I wanted to see him strut his stuff."

Her smile was automatic. "I'm glad. I wish he knew you were here."

"He will. By the way, a team can only score at bat."

"Ah. And when they get two more outs, we can bat."

"Right." He turned his attention to the game, where the pitcher had already thrown one ball. Quietly he added, "Then we'll really see what the kid's made of."

Clarice immediately tensed. Her son had to face yet another test? She gulped back a protest, reminding herself that Trenton wanted to do this, even if she couldn't imagine why, and fixed her attention on the field. Her hands were clenched around the edge of the rough bleacher bench, her concentration so intense that she failed to notice the indulgent look Bolton sent her way or feel the feather-light touch of his fingertips skimming her knuckles.

Actually, it was a long while before Trenton came to bat, and by the time he did, his team was ahead by a score of two to one. The umpire had called a ball and two strikes and Clarice was gnawing a fingernail when Trenton stepped back from the plate, removed the batting helmet, and wiped his forehead on his sleeve. She started praying again, only to be interrupted by Bolton pulling her hand away from her mouth. He folded it into his own, grasping it tightly.

"Lighten up," he ordered softly. "He's going to do fine, and it's just a game, after all."

The fat guy behind her yelled, "Get it together, kid! Don't let us down!"

Clarice yanked her head around. "Do you mind? He's got enough pressure on him already!"

He glowered at her. "Don't you know encouragement when you hear it, lady?"

Encouragement! She opened her mouth to tell him what he could do with his encouragement, but Bolton slid an arm around her shoulders and turned her forcefully to the front.

"Let's concentrate on the game," he murmured.

She saw that Trenton had again stepped up to the plate, and her mouth went dry. He hefted the bat, bending slightly at the waist. The pitcher stared longer than seemed necessary, but Trenton merely continued to get the feel of the bat. The pitcher drew up—It seemed so unfair, a grown man pitching to a mere boy!—drew back, and... The ball cracked against the bat. Clarice screamed and lunged to her feet. Bolton's arm had tightened convulsively about her shoulders. The bat went flying and so did Trenton. She was jumping up and down. Bolton was jumping up and down beside her, the arm locked tightly about her had slid down to her waist, pinning her arms to her sides. Trent stomped first base and plunged on. Bolton groaned. The guy behind them started yelling, "No! No! Go back! Go back!"

Clarice caught her breath. One frantic look told her an outfielder with a particularly strong arm was about to throw her son out at second base, but Trenton couldn't possibly know. He had his head down, arms and legs flying. The ball whipped toward the second baseman. He had his glove up, his knees flexed. Trenton plowed into him like a runaway locomotive, knocking him flat and planting a staggering foot on the base bag. The ball burned by his head and plopped into the dirt. The umpire chopped his arms through the air and called, "Safe!"

Clarice's knees buckled. She'd have collapsed if not for Bolton's arms clamped around her, squeezing the breath out of her lungs. He was yelling in her ear and hopping up and down. The guy behind her started pounding on her shoulders.

"Way to go, kid! Way to go! That little sucker can run, lady! Got him an arm, too!"

She managed a weak "Thank you," before Bolton pulled her down on the bench next to him.

"Oh, man, that was close! My heart stopped when he went for second base! Man, oh, man, what a play! I told you he'd do well. I told you!"

She felt sick, her stomach rumbling ominously, but she forced her mouth up into some semblance of a smile and swallowed air. Gradually she became aware of Bolton's arm now draped casually about her shoulders. Disturbed, she edged carefully to the side, crowding the woman next to her, who gave her a frowning look. Clarice smiled lamely and settled into place. A moment later, Bolton removed his arm and proceeded to applaud encouragement to the boy at bat. He didn't look at her, and she didn't say anything, but something told her that he had been very aware of her discomfort. She felt a moment of intense regret, then buoyed. If they were going to be friends, they were both going to have to learn to deal with the limitations of friendship. He knew how she stood on the matter. If he couldn't accept that... She abandoned the thought and concentrated on the game.

Not many moments later, the batter got a good solid hit that drove Trenton in for what would turn out to be the final score. The euphoria was hardly waning when Bolton's beeper went off. He glanced down, frowning, then turned to her apologetically.

"Gotta go. I'm pretty sure he knew I was here, but you tell him how proud I am of him, just in case. All right?" He stepped down onto the bleacher below.

She tamped down an unwelcome spurt of disappointment. "Sure. I hope everything works out for the best at the hospital."

"No doubt about it," he said softly, "one of the rewards guaranteed by faith." Then he stepped down twice more and hurriedly strode out of sight.

The woman upon whose space she had encroached turned to her then. Her gaze was friendly, inquisitive. "That's the preacher, isn't it?"

Clarice felt a tremor of warning. "Yes."

The woman smiled. "He's a good guy. My brother was out of work last year, lost his house. Preacher Charles found them a place and got the church to pay part of the rent until things picked up again. Had my brother helping out around the church building, you know, so it wasn't like charity. Good guy."

"Very," Clarice said, her alarm replaced by an odd surge of pride. "H-he's a friend of my son's," she explained almost defensively.

The woman's smile broadened. "The boy who ran in that last score, right?"

Clarice smiled in return. "That's right."

"Good player," the woman said. "Wish he was on the other team."

Clarice thanked her as she turned away. Bolton was a good guy, and Trenton was a good player—and she was a good mother, or trying to be. Trying very hard to be. She folded her hands in her lap and watched the waning few moments of the game, ignoring the loneliness she suddenly felt there in those bleachers surrounded by dozens of others with whom she obviously had at least one thing in common. She wondered about that family at the hospital. Bolton would be a comfort to them, a strengthening friend in time of need. She thought about calling later to find out what had happened. But no, it wasn't any concern of hers. Bolton hadn't even mentioned a name. He might well interpret her empathy as concern for him.

She grimaced. This friendship business was more complicated than she had realized. If only he hadn't made his interest in other areas so very obvious, and yet, she knew she was going to take that kiss out of its memory box and turn it over and over in her mind for a long time to come.

The umpire called the final out, and the game was over. Trenton's team whooped and hollered. The coach let them celebrate a few moments, then herded them into a line for after-game handshakes with the other team. Clarice strolled to the chain-link barrier that protected the spectators from wild pitches and pop-up balls. She listened to the comments being made by those milling about her.

"Good game."

"That new shortstop's a whiz."

"We'll get them next time."

"Be interesting to watch that new kid and see what he does from here on out."

"Eric could play that well if you'd spend some time with him."

"Holy cow! There's just so many hours in a day, you know."

She stopped listening. So many hours in a day. People hurting and dying and out of work. Little boys without fathers. One caring man with a beeper hooked onto his belt, and that man was her friend. She made a sudden decision. All right, it was complicated, but she was putting her doubts away. It was bound to be worth it. What were a few complications when one considered the rewards of friendship with a man like Bolton Charles? He was a man who would never say, when a need was pointed out to him, that there were only so many hours in a day.

She was taken off guard when her son ran up to her, his face split by a megasmile. "Hey, look at you! I guess all that dirt is a result of a really good game, huh?" Clarice said.

"We won!"

"I know!"

"Where's Bolton? I saw him here."

"He had to go see some people at the hospital, Trenton. Somebody's really sick."

"Okay," he said lightly. "That's cool."

She knew he didn't mean that it was "cool" that somebody was ill. She turned him toward the parking area, and they started off toward the car. "He saw you score," she told him.

"Yeah? That's great!" He swaggered a bit. "'Course, we'd have won anyway without it."

"True, but you still played well. Bolton told me you would, you know?"

He beamed up at her. "He told me that, too, but I was really nervous."

She didn't say that he hadn't been any more nervous than she had been. They reached the car.

He opened the door and tossed his glove into the back seat. "Can I call him?"

She stopped in the act of fishing her keys out of her purse. "Call Bolton?"

He nodded. "I want to tell him it worked, that thing about stepping in front of the runner."

So that was where he'd gotten the move! She should have known. She smiled. "We'll try," she said. "But he might be at the hospital until quite late."

Trenton shrugged. "No big deal. I can tell him tomorrow."

But he didn't have to wait until tomorrow. Bolton showed up on their doorstep not two hours later, a pained, apologetic expression upon his face.

"I hope I haven't come by too late," he said wearily.

He looked so in need of succor that Clarice's heart wrung. Panicked by the strength of her reaction, she very nearly closed the door in his face. Trenton, however, was passing through the entry, wearing his undershorts and bathrobe, having come from the kitchen where he'd gobbled down a bedtime snack. He ran to the door.

"Bolt!"

The minister's face instantly brightened. "Hey, sport!" He went down on one knee and received an enthusiastic hug. "I just had to come by and tell you what a great game you had tonight. You were the star, pal! I was bustin' my buttons!"

Clarice clutched her fist in the center of her chest. She had never seen her son so happy. He basked unself-consciously in the glow of Bolton's pride and praise. There were no deprecating remarks about not having made the winning score, no carefully solemnized gazes, only the joy of accomplishment. She watched him put his arms around Bolton's neck once more. Bolton closed his eyes and squeezed the boy with such obviously heartfelt affection that Clarice felt the beginnings of tears sharpened and heated by sheer jealousy. She forced aside the emotion with some effort and no little shame. If this was what her son needed, this was what her son was going to get, and she could at least be gracious about it. She put on a forced smile.

"Would you like to come in for a few minutes?"

Bolton glanced up at her. "If you're sure it's no bother."

"No bother. Why don't we go into the living room?"

He ruffled Trenton's hair and pushed up to his full height. "All right. Thank you."

She led the way through double doors of carved cherry, jumping into this hostess thing with both feet. "Would you like some refreshments? Trenton was just having some milk and cookies in the kitchen, and I'm sure there's plenty more."

His chuckle brought her back to her senses. "Milk and cookies? Something tells me it's been a while since you entertained anyone over twelve years old."

She felt herself blushing. "Oh. I—I'll make a pot of coffee and—"

"No, don't bother. I had a bite to eat at the hospital." His smile negated the gruffness of his tone.

The hospital. Her thoughts turned instantly to those with problems far more painful than hers. "I wanted to ask you, how did it go there?"

He glanced down at the boy at his side. "Why don't we talk about that later?" he said lightly.

She looked at her son and blanched. "Of course." Of all the idiotic things she could have done, discussing a recent death in front of Trenton would have capped them all. She tamped down her irritation with herself and stepped forward. "It's time you were in bed, young man. You need a good night's rest after the workout you've had."

"But, Mom," the boy pleaded, "Bolt's here."

"Your mom's right, Trent," Bolton said. "Tell you what, if it's okay, I'll go up with you and see you settled in." He looked to Clarice for permission and received it by way of an almost curt nod. Trenton beamed, absolutely delighted to have Bolton with him for a few minutes more. "Up we go, pal." Bolton turned him back toward the entry foyer and the staircase.

Clarice could hear her son's excited voice recalling the highlights of the game and Bolton's much deeper comments. She walked across the room to the sturdy reproduction Victorian chaise known as a fainting couch and sat down, but five minutes later she was wandering aimlessly among the Federal-style armchairs, Empire commodes and Duncan Phyfe tables with which her late mother-in-law had crammed the large, dark room. Clarice thought for the millionth time that, given leave, she'd cart half this stuff out, replace the heavy velvet draperies with painted shutters, apply a pale pickled finish to the mahogany paneling and bring in a pair of large, overstuffed sofas covered in bold stripes and bright flowers. It was wishful thinking, of course. Wallis would never allow her to "tinker" with his room or any other in the house through which he might pass in a week's time. For some reason that irritated her more than usual tonight. For some reason everything irritated her more than usual tonight. She went back to the chaise and sat down again.

Nearly half an hour passed before Bolton rejoined her. When he did, he was whistling softly some nearly forgotten tune, his countenance much brightened since his arrival. He greeted her with a smile and a jaunty bow, saying, "I think we've got the makings of a sports commentator on our hands. He was compelled to analyze the game throw by throw before we could settle down to our good-night prayers and pack it in."

We. Our. Clarice felt a streak of raw possessiveness. Who did he think he was, laying claim to her son like that? The next instant, however, sanity prevailed. He was a friend, a needed friend, and Trenton absolutely doted on him. Certainly he'd made no effort to relive the game with *her*. She told herself that it was a "guy" thing and made a stately rise to her feet, unaware of the stoniness of her face.

"I'll see you out," she said with exaggerated graciousness, but as she swept by him, he grabbed her by the upper arms, turning her back to face him.

"What's wrong?"

Wrong? She opened her mouth to snap at him, but how could she tell him what she was feeling—the jealousy, the possessiveness, the panic? She swallowed down an acidic reply and drew a calming breath through gently flaring nostrils. "It's late," she said stiltedly. "You've had a difficult evening. My son kept you too long."

Brown eyes plumbed hers. "I thought you were concerned about what went on at the hospital."

She dropped her gaze and stepped back, out of his grasp. "Yes, of course. You never did tell me the family's name."

"Caswell," he said flatly.

Her gaze flickered up. "Surely not those people with the bakery."

His lips flattened regretfully. "The same. It was his mother."

She wished he had not told her. It was one thing to sympathize with people unknown, but the acquaintance, however slight, made it more personal. She sighed, knowing she would write a note of condolence. The Caswells had baked Trenton's birthday cake every year since his birth, and she remembered quite clearly the dozens of warm crusty buns in Caswell Bakery bags that had arrived unordered at Revere House after the deaths of her mother-in-law and husband. That would have been arranged through the church, of course. No doubt they were members. She cleared away a lump in her throat and sank down in the nearest chair.

"How did it happen?" she asked softly.

Bolton took a chair opposite her. "She had been ill a very long time and required constant care. In the end, she went softly in her sleep. It was a blessing in many ways, but..." His voice trailed off, signaling unpleasantness.

Clarice bit her lip, struggling with the conflicting desires to know the whole of it and spare herself the worst. The former won. She lifted her chin. "But what?"

"I wouldn't want you to think I'm gossiping."

"I won't."

"It's just so helpful to be able to share this kind of thing with someone who cares."

She did care. She didn't want to, but she did. She steeled herself. "Go on."

He sighed and folded his hands together in his lap. "Mr. Caswell has a sister. She is not what I would call 'spiritually mature,' and there were conflicts with her mother." He spread his hands ineffectually. "It's so difficult to accept the death of a loved one with whom we've had quarrels we've never mended. The regret comes too late. We see our folly and can't correct it. Our grief is compounded by guilt." He sighed. "What do you say to someone whose last words to her mother were tainted with hate and resentment?"

Is was a rhetorical question, a fact for which Clarice would have given thanks had her mind grasped it, but instead she was hearing words from her past, bitter, angry words. *You don't love me! You own me! I'm another possession, like the horse and the corral and the fast cars! I wish to God I'd never married you!* She closed her eyes, as if that could shut out the remembered sound of her own voice, and when she opened them again, Bolton was there, crouched beside her.

"Clarice?"

"Oh." She caught her breath, her hand going to her mouth. "It's nothing! It's..."

He took her other hand in his. "I'm so sorry I've upset you."

She wanted suddenly to fall on his neck and weep, but then she thought of having his arms around her and his mouth hovering near hers, and she leapt to her feet in panic. "Please go now. I'm very tired. I—I don't want to talk anymore." She was being unbelievably rude, but she couldn't help it. Another moment and she would burst into tears—or worse. His face hardened, and she watched him willfully relax his expression then get slowly to his feet.

"Good night," he whispered raggedly, and then he strode from the room and across the foyer. A moment later she heard the brass door knocker rattle as he closed the door roughly behind him.

She put her hands to her face and dropped back into the chair. Dear God, what was happening to her? An old lady she had never even known had died gently in her sleep and she was weeping into her hands and longing for the comfort of the one man who would be the ruin of her.

Chapter Five

Clarice signed her name at the bottom of the check and paused a moment, feeling absurdly satisfied. The kind of pleasure she took these days from paying her own bills might seem absolutely macabre to anyone who didn't realize how fierce a battle she'd fought for the privilege. Wallis Revere had held the financial reins for so long that he'd been deeply offended by her determination to open her own bank account and handle her own expenses. Convincing her few creditors to bill her directly rather than sending invoices to her father-in-law's accountant had proved the real battle, however. She had not realized that she'd had no real credit standing of her own. It had been necessary to prove that she was entitled to income of her own from her husband's estate, all of which was controlled by Wallis. Then, she had to contend with the knowledge that the income was far too small to pay all of her expenses.

If Wallis did not provide her with a home, pay the utilities and buy the groceries, her situation would be hopeless.

It was that knowledge that finally reconciled Wallis to the new system. He still held a great deal of control over her finances, but at least she had taken *some* of that power into her own hands. She was determined to take more. Come fall, she intended to be enrolled in some sort of educational program designed to make her suitable for gainful employment. She shuddered at the thought of Wallis's reaction to *that,* but she was determined, and nothing was going to change her mind—nothing and no one.

She ripped the check out of the book, folded it and inserted it into an envelope. She was sealing the envelope when Teresa knocked and opened the door to the sitting room.

"Pardon, Miss Clarice. Someone here to see you, *por favor.*"

Someone to see her? Her slender brows rose at the unexpected announcement, then she bit her lip. It couldn't be anyone but Bolton Charles. Her heart pounded at the knowledge, but she took a steely grip upon herself and lifted her chin imperiously. "Tell him I'm out," she said flatly. To her surprise, Teresa edged farther into the room, hands twisting in her apron.

"Pardon, Miss Clarice. It's not him," she said plaintively. "It's her, Señora Fro...uh—" She broke off, shrugging. Teresa was quite hopeless with names, but apparently this visitor was a woman, not Bolton Charles.

Clarice sat up straighter, trying to digest this surprising piece of news. What woman would be visiting her? Well, there was only one way to find out. She pushed her chair back from the little desk and got up. "All right, Teresa, I'll be right down. Where is she?"

Teresa looked momentarily abashed. "I put her in the living room."

Clarice frowned. That meant the poor woman was standing uneasily in the foyer as they spoke. "Hurry up and put her in a chair," she said more sharply than she'd intended. "I'll be down in a moment."

Teresa nodded and slipped away. Clarice tried to think, her gaze fluttering to the floor. Oh! She was still wearing her bedroom slippers. She hurried into her room, stepped out of the slippers beside the bed, and went to the closet for a pair of beige, fringed slip-ons. Her feet safely encased in proper leather, she tucked in the tail of her white cotton blouse more neatly, smoothed her khaki A-line skirt, then pulled a matching vest from the closet. She shrugged into it and buttoned it up. After pulling a brush through her hair, she was ready to face this unknown female visitor.

She wondered whom she might find waiting for her in the living room. Silently she proposed and discarded several names. The sad truth was that she didn't really have any friends. Her late husband had so completely commanded her life from the time of their first meeting until his death that she hadn't had room for simple friendship. In the years since his death, she had lived her life virtually within the walls of Revere House, focusing almost entirely upon her son, and she had been satisfied with that. She had been satisfied, that is, until Trenton had started attending school full-time. Since then, her dissatisfaction—and her vision— had grown. She realized now what a barren, stifling existence they had led. But none of this offered the least clue to the identity of the woman in the living room.

Clarice swept into the room, needing for some reason to appear busy and competent and in control. The woman sitting primly upon the fainting couch was a complete stranger. She was a little plump, with soft brown hair piled loosely upon her head and carefully composed features. She wore a navy pantsuit with a nautical flavor about the double-breasted jacket trimmed in white. Her hands nervously clutched a small navy handbag in her lap. Clarice stepped forward, smiling in an effort to put her unknown visitor at ease.

"Hello, I'm Clarice Revere."

The woman got quickly to her feet. "Mrs. Revere, my name's Andrea Forrest."

The name meant nothing to Clarice, but she motioned for the woman to reclaim her seat and pulled a chair around to face the couch. She settled down, patience in her every movement, and crossed her legs at the ankles. "Now then, Mrs. Forrest—I assume it's Mrs.—"

Andrea Forrest flushed. "Yes, of course. I should have said that, but this is such an informal call. I mean, I hoped...that is, I wish you'd call me Andrea."

Clarice smiled again, carefully concealing her surprise. "All right, and you must call me Clarice, naturally. Now then, Andrea, how can I help you?"

Andrea seemed momentarily taken aback. "Well, you can't!" she finally blurted, and the next instant her face colored to an alarming shade of mottled red. Clarice sat forward, suddenly concerned for her mysterious guest, but then Andrea Forrest started to laugh, silently at first, then with muffled, strangled chuckles and finally with hearty, cleansing guffaws that made Clarice giggle, as well. "I'm sorry," the woman said, wiping her eyes with the backs of her hands. "It's just that I'm so out of my depth here." She waved a hand and glanced around her. "I mean, this big old house and all these fine things, they're kind of..."

"Intimidating?" Clarice supplied helpfully.

"Intimidating," Andrea Forrest concurred. "But interesting," she added quickly. As if in demonstration, her hand fell upon the piece of furniture beneath her. "What is this thing called, if you don't mind my asking?"

Clarice disciplined a smile and managed a shrug. "It's just a kind of chaise longue," she said. "It's called a fainting couch. I'm told that is a replica of one from Victorian England. Someone famous once fainted on it—the original, I mean.''

"Ah." Andrea Forrest looked down at the thing in puzzlement, as if trying to figure out why anyone would want such a thing.

Clarice put a hand over her mouth, suppressing a gush of fresh giggles. "Awful, isn't it?" she said impulsively.

Andrea shot her a surprised look, then a smile wiggled across her generous mouth. "It's certainly not what I'd want in my living room."

Suddenly they were both laughing again, and it was a very companionable feeling. When they calmed this time, Clarice was the one wiping her eyes. "I've always hated that thing," she admitted happily. "My late mother-in-law was into antiques when she decorated this room, and her taste was nevér very practical, poor dear."

"Consider yourself lucky," Andrea said. "*My* mother-in-law's taste runs to dairies. I'm serious. She made a lamp out of a butter churn and had her living room sofa reupholstered in what looks like the hide of an old Guernsey cow."

That brought fresh gales of giggles and stifled snickering. "Forgive me," Clarice said, struggling for composure. "That was unbelievably ill-mannered of me."

"Not at all!" Andrea protested. "Just a bit of fun, but you would feel that way. Pastor said you were a sweet one, and I can see he's right."

Pastor? Clarice stiffened involuntarily. "You mean Bolton Charles sent you here?"

Andrea nodded. "Said you were interested in Bible study but needed some encouragement. Asked me to stop by and make a personal invitation."

She should have known. When one's circle of friends was as severely limited as her own, it shouldn't be too difficult to figure out these things. The only inexplicable aspect was the keen sense of disappointment she felt. She cleared her throat, struggling for a light tone. "You really shouldn't have bothered," she said.

"No bother!" Andrea Forrest exclaimed. "Oh, no, I'm delighted to make this call. We've always got our feelers out for new members for our Bible study class, you know. We're always ready to reach out. Besides," she confessed, "I've wanted to see inside this house for an age. I jumped at the chance to come here. It's just that the Reveres are well-off folk, and that makes a simple farmer's wife like me a bit uncertain, you see. But you sure are everything Pastor said you were, kind and gracious and likable. Very pretty, he said, too," she confided with a wiggle of an unplucked brow.

Clarice caught her breath, shaken by the pronounced thrill of pleasure Andrea's words brought her. Bolton thought her "very pretty". Resolutely she pushed the thought and feelings away. She squirmed in her chair, searching for the least offensive way to put this. "I'm, ah, not sure that I really am interested—at this time. The thing is, my father-in-law likes to have private services here."

"I know what you mean," Andrea said chummily. "My father was the same way. He was kind of the controlling type, you know, but he meant well. He thought organized religion was unnatural. Then he got sick, and this woman came to see my mother at the hospital where he was, and she found out what we needed, somebody to see after the kids and food in the house and help with the chores, and the church took care of it. The women, they came and took turns caring for all us kids. There's eight of us, you know, and me smack in the middle. And every day somebody was dropping off food, and they were sending out all these young men to help with the place." She paused to grin.

"One of them I married, and he's a fine God-fearing man, my husband. Anyway, without the church, we'd have had to go on welfare, and I imagine my daddy would have died of mortification over that. He still says organized religion's unnatural, but he goes every Sunday, rain or shine."

Clarice could only smile. Andrea Forrest was nothing if not open and friendly. "I don't think my father-in-law is likely to become a regular attender," she said, "but my little boy goes very faithfully. Bolton, er, Reverend Charles has seen to that."

Andrea nodded conspiratorially. "I know your son. He's a sweet one, too, so well behaved and polite. Must be hard on a boy to do without a father."

Clarice squirmed uncomfortably. "Yes, but then he doesn't remember his father."

"Now that's sad," Andrea declared. "But never mind. You'll marry again one day, pretty little thing like you."

Clarice gasped and tried to cover it with a cough. "I, um, haven't really thought about it. I don't, um, get out much."

Andrea waved a hand dismissively. "Oh, we'll take care of that. We don't just study Bible, you know. We fellowship—dinners, parties. We even go bowling and play softball, fishing trips—all kinds of stuff. But that's not the best part, really. We're *there* for one another. Know what I mean? Like that time my father was in the hospital. We try to help out every way from praying to paying the rent. Whatever's needed. It's like...family. That's just what it is, a family, and if you can't praise God for that on a Sunday morning, why, you're to be pitied." She put a hand to her mouth in dismay. "Oh, not you personally. I was speaking in general, you know. That is, I didn't mean ... Well, I did, but not..." She started to chuckle again. "Open mouth, insert foot. I swear, it's a wonder I don't get hoof-and-mouth disease!"

Clarice was laughing, too. It seemed a natural occurrence around Andrea Forrest. She was surprised to find that
she liked this woman immensely. Spending time with her
would be quite entertaining, whatever the setting, and she
was tempted, deeply tempted, to take her up on her invitation. And why not? She had a right to friends of her own,
didn't she. *Family* of her own? It struck her suddenly that
there were people out there who would be willing to help her,
people whom she could help in turn, people who might grow
fond of her, of whom she might grow fond. The confines of
her life could be pushed back, perhaps a great deal, and
Trenton's with it. She made a sudden decision.

"Won't you come?" Andrea Forrest was saying. "We're
all women in our thirties, all married or have been, all with
kids. Some of us have been through some pretty tough
times, and some of us have had charmed lives—not me,
mind you, but one or two. We share what we want to and
keep private what we want to, and most importantly, we
care. That's what it's all about, really. Caring. Why, I don't
know how you can resist us!" she quipped.

"I can't," Clarice said firmly, delighted with the way her
new friend's face lit up. "If the rest of the class is anything
like you, I'm going to be very happy."

Andrea jumped up and hurried over to give Clarice a
bone-crushing hug. "Aw, honey, you're going to fit in like
a chick in a brood. I'm so excited I could cry."

"Oh, don't do that!" Clarice exclaimed, getting to her
feet.

Andrea laughed and flicked her hand. "I cry about everything. My husband won't even take me to a movie for
fear I'll weep all over his shirtsleeve."

They laughed together over that, then Andrea said she
just had to leave. She'd dropped the kids off at the pool on

her way over, and swimming lessons were bound to be finished by now.

"Your boy has to come out to the farm and see all the little babies we've got," she enthused on her way to the door.
"There's nothing cuter than animal babies. We'll fix something up on Sunday. You take care, darlin', and I'll see you
then." She kissed Clarice on the cheek and quit the house in
a streak of navy blue.

Clarice stood on the doorstep and waved as the big old car
rumbled down the drive. She still wanted to laugh and could
hardly believe what had transpired. She had a friend. Correction—she now had two friends; for whatever else he
might be, Bolton Charles was surely that. And he thought
her "very pretty."

On Tuesday evening of the following week, Bolton took
Trenton and a friend from the baseball team to a movie.
Afterward, Trenton's new friend spent the night at Revere
House, and Bolton came in for a while to report on the
movie. He was talkative, relaxed and engaging. He asked if
Andrea Forrest had been to see her, and upon receiving a
positive answer, spoke very fondly of the woman. Clarice
had to agree with his description of Andrea as funny,
friendly and "salt of the earth." Bolton didn't ask if she'd
decided to attend Sunday morning Bible study, but only said
that he was glad she and Andrea had got on.

"She'll make you a good friend," he said firmly.

Clarice smiled. "Yes, I know. I must thank you for putting her on to me."

He waved a hand dismissively and rose to leave. After
he'd gone, she found that she wished he'd stayed a little
longer.

Bolton showed up for the baseball game on Thursday
while the teams were still warming up and stayed until the

last hurrah had faded into silence. Trenton's team lost by one run, but Trenton himself played a fine game and enough people told him so that he didn't seem to feel too bad about the loss. After the game, Bolton took several of the boys for ice cream, saying he had good friends in the business. Later, when he brought Trenton home, he just dropped the boy off at the door, saw him inside and went on his way. Clarice resolutely ignored the disappointment she felt—until she lay alone in her empty bed. Then, for the first time, she let herself dream about what might be.

It did not take long, however, for her to realize that even in her dreams, she and Bolton did not fit. She was no more cut out to be a minister's wife than she was cut out to be... Unfortunately, she didn't know *what* she was cut out to be. She had tried very hard to be the kind of wife that Trenton's father had wanted, but she had not been happy doing so, and she knew that he had not been completely satisfied with her efforts, either. She had comforted herself for several years with the thought that she was, though a failure as a wife, a very good mother. Certainly, she had always been devoted to her son, and yet she had eventually come to see that being the object of one's devotion was not necessarily everything that a growing boy needed.

So she had not been a raging success as a mother, either—but she still could be. She was learning. And come fall she was going to point herself in a whole new direction. She was not going to live off Wallis Revere's grudging largess any longer than absolutely necessary. If only she could find the direction in which she was meant to go.... With that in mind, she stole a page from Bolton Charles's book and resorted to prayer, lengthy, beseeching, desperate prayer. Afterward, feeling comforted if not enlightened, she fell asleep with the thought that she could enlist Andrea Forrest's prayers in her behalf as well.

On Sunday morning, Clarice donned a tailored coat dress with princess seams. Double-breasted and short-sleeved, with notched lapels and rolled collar, it was both elegant and cool, and the delicate mint-green color brought out the reddish highlights of her pale hair and the mossy shade of her eyes. When matched with stockings and shoes of the same hue, the dress made her feel exceptionally well turned out. So much so, that she felt quite lighthearted even as she dealt with Wallis's grumbling displeasure at her defection. She promised him that she would join him for their usual Bible reading and prayer later in the day, but this morning, she told him firmly, she and Trenton were attending study and services at the church. When she attempted to kiss him on the cheek in hopes of softening the blow to his authority, he jerked his head away, snapping at her to get out. She did so calmly, her resignation affecting not in the least her delight at having taken this step.

Trenton was waiting in the entry hall, his softly bound Bible rolled and stuffed into a pocket in his suit jacket. Clarice clucked her tongue, pulled the Bible from the pocket, thrust it into his hands and corrected the part in his hair with her thumbnail, smoothing the errant hairs with her fingertips. She stepped back to look him over and noted that the sleeves of his jacket were not quite long enough. The waistband of his trousers was snug, too. She was going to have to buy him a new suit, and her resources were already stretched quite to the limit. Independence had its negatives. She wondered if the garments could be let out and decided to take the matter to Teresa later.

They walked through the house to the garage door. Jack, the part-time gardener, was in the garage fetching his wheelbarrow. Clarice had given him permission to keep it there rather than in the gardening shed at the far end of the property; the shed was located in a little hollow that made it difficult for the old man to move the wheelbarrow in and out. Jack had made the same request of Wallis and been denied, but Clarice had decided that what Wallis didn't know wouldn't hurt him in this instance. Wallis never came into the garage. The only time he ever left the house, which was seldom indeed, he had the van brought around to the front in order to accommodate his wheelchair. She smiled at Jack as she put Trenton into the front seat of her car.

"Working on Sunday, Jack?"

The old man stopped and straightened, a hand pressed to the small of his back. "Now you know I'm Seventh-Day Adventist, Miss Clarice. I worship on Saturday."

"I had forgotten," she admitted sheepishly.

"No matter," he said kindly. "Now where are you off to, all dressed so pretty?"

"Well, thank you, Jack. I'm on my way to church, of course."

He seemed shocked. "I thought Mr. Wallis didn't attend services anymore."

"He doesn't," Clarice said matter-of-factly.

Old Jack stared, then shook his head, grinning. "So it's finally come," he said, "and high time it is, too. Before long you'll be leaving us for good, I reckon."

"I imagine that's some time away yet," she said lightly, walking around the car, but he shook his grizzled head.

"No, you have that look about you, that look of a woman with a purpose. Before you know it, you'll be falling in love again."

Clarice stopped, her keys in her hand. "Why on earth would you say that?"

He chuckled. "Why, cause it's the way of the world. It's the natural thing, you know, as opposed to a pretty young gal trying to bury herself with her husband. That's not healthy, to my way of thinking, but now look at you. You're starting to live again, Miss Clarice. You're ready to let yourself be happy again. Love will just naturally follow."

Love? The very idea shook her right down to the soles of her feet. Was it *natural* to surrender her fledgling independence to another man? Was it *healthy* to put herself at the beck and call of another tyrant? Tyrant? Was that what her husband had become to her? Or had she so closely tied him up in her head with Wallis that she could no longer tell the difference between the two? She pushed away such thoughts. Love was an illusion, a trap. All that mattered was making a happy life for herself and her son. Today was one more step along that path. That's all she had to think about right now. She gripped the keys more tightly and relaxed her face into a smile.

"I would never have pegged you for a romantic," she said teasingly to the old man, "and all this talk about love is going to make me late to church."

"Wouldn't want to do that," he said, old eyes twinkling. "Church is a good place to find a good man."

Clarice nearly dropped her keys as she fitted them into the ignition. A good man. Did he know? Could that old tease know...? No, of course not. What an absurd idea. There was nothing to know about her and Bolton Charles. He was a friend. A kiss meant nothing, not a kiss that would never be repeated anyway. And she wasn't going to church to "find" him. She was going for herself and her son. She was going for Andrea Forrest. She was going for God, because it was right and proper to worship Him and to study His Word. She was going because it was the next logical step along the long road to real independence, to taking back her own life and giving her son a life of his own. She started up the engine and put the transmission into gear. Love was not in the picture, and in truth, she didn't think it ever had been.

He was standing on the sidewalk when they pulled up next to the curb, a large green-and-yellow umbrella shielding him from the light rain falling from a pearl-gray sky. He laughed and hopped out of the way as two redheaded, freckle-faced boys leapt from an old station wagon in front of Clarice's car and tore up the walk toward the safety of the church foyer. Bolton hurried over to the passenger side of the station wagon and shielded the door as a heavily pregnant young woman with golden blond hair eased herself out. His hand protectively cupped about her elbow, Bolton escorted the young woman around the car, helped her up over the curb and waited until she'd popped her own umbrella to shield herself from the rain. Umbrellas jostling, the woman leaned close, strained upward and gave Bolton a peck on the cheek. The driver's side window of the station wagon lowered and a man with a military-style haircut, presumably the young woman's husband, stuck his head out and shouted, "Hey, Rev, I'd watch it if I were you. It might be catching!"

"What's that?" Bolton shouted back.

"Twins!" the man yelled, pulling back inside to roll up his window.

Bolton gaped at the young woman's distended stomach. Clarice saw her laugh and nod her head, at which point Bolton dropped his umbrella and clasped both arms around the woman's shoulders. She laughingly pushed him away, her much smaller umbrella doing a poor job of shielding his big frame. He snatched up his own shelter again and after a few moments, he left her and came to help Trenton from the car.

"Sorry about the delay," he said, laughter imbuing his voice with a lightness she had never heard. He glanced up as another car pulled up behind Clarice's. "Out you go, pal. Don't step in this puddle." He tugged Trenton away from the car and closed the door.

Clarice felt an immediate stab of resentment. He hadn't even asked if she was going to stay, had hardly even acknowledged her. She watched him usher her son up onto the sidewalk and down its length to the relative dryness of the roof overhang. Trenton pointed back toward the car, turned and hurried inside the building. Before Bolton's gaze could find her, she started the car forward, tires spraying water as she drove toward the parking area. For a few seconds, she debated driving right past the turnoff to the street, but at the last moment she turned the car and pulled into the first empty space she found. Bolton Charles was no part of why she had chosen to attend church this morning, she reminded herself, and if he had given up on her, so much the better.

Ignoring her smarting feelings, she reached under her seat for the small telescoping umbrella she kept there, only to remember that she had moved it to the trunk with the onset of summer weather. She groaned and leaned her forehead against the steering wheel. Maybe God was trying to tell her something. Maybe this was a mistake after all. And maybe she would not drown if she just got out and opened up the trunk. *No, but everyone would see you with your hair wilting and plastered to your head.* She knew without putting his name to it that the *one* among *everyone* whom she really didn't want to see her like that was Bolton Charles, and she instinctively rejected such a dangerous emotion.

Determined again, she took her keys in hand, clutched her handbag beneath her arm and pushed open the car door. The rain was coming down in fine, even drops, just heavier than a mist, but enough had fallen already to create puddles in every small hollow or depression in the asphalt. She stretched her leg out to avoid just such a puddle and felt her skirt hike up. As she struggled out of the car, her skirt hiked higher still, but she didn't worry about it, thinking she was quite alone—until Bolton Charles, umbrella aloft, trotted around the end of the car situated next to her and came to an abrupt halt.

For an instant, while the rain came down gently upon her head, Clarice was too stunned to move, but then she realized what he was looking at and grabbed at the hem of her skirt. That seemed to get him moving again, for he was suddenly standing over her, one hand holding up the umbrella, the other reaching for her arm.

"Let me—" he began, but she shook him off and leapt to her feet, even though it meant planting both shoes squarely in the center of the puddle she had been trying to avoid in the first place.

"I can do it myself!" she snapped, only to hear him chortle. He sounded like he was choking to death on a chuckle, and she wanted to poke him with her fist for it, but the sound had an oddly endearing quality about it, too, especially as his dark eyes sparkled with a very serious twinkle.

"What are you embarrassed about?" he asked after a moment. "You've got great legs."

FREE BOOKS!

FREE GIFTS!

PLAY THE "LUCKY 7" SLOT MACHINE GAME!

AND YOU COULD GET
FREE BOOKS PLUS A FREE
VICTORIAN PICTURE
FRAME!

NO COST! NO OBLIGATION TO BUY!
NO PURCHASE NECESSARY!

PLAY "LUCKY 7"
AND GET AS MANY AS FIVE FREE GIFTS . . .
HOW TO PLAY:

1. With a coin, carefully scratch off the silver box at the right. This makes you eligible to receive two or more free books, and possibly another gift, depending on what is revealed beneath the scratch-off area.

2. Send back this card and you'll receive brand-new Silhouette Romance™ novels. These books have a cover price of $2.75 each, but they are yours to keep absolutely free.

3. There's no catch. You're under no obligation to buy anything. We charge nothing—ZERO—for your first shipment. And you don't have to make any minimum number of purchases—not even one!

4. The fact is thousands of readers enjoy receiving books by mail from the Silhouette Reader Service™ months before they're available in stores. They like the convenience of home delivery and they love our discount prices!

5. We hope that after receiving your free books you'll want to remain a subscriber. But the choice is yours—to continue or cancel, anytime at all! So why not take us up on our invitation, with no risk of any kind. You'll be glad you did!

This lovely Victorian pewter-finish miniature is perfect for displaying a treasured photograph. And it's yours FREE as added thanks for giving our Reader Service a try!

PLAY "LUCKY 7"

**Just scratch off the silver box with a coin.
Then check below to see which gifts you get.**

YES! I have scratched off the silver box. Please send me all the gifts for which I qualify. I understand I am under no obligation to purchase any books, as explained on the back and on the opposite page.

215 CIS AK9W
(U-SIL-R-11/93)

NAME

ADDRESS   APT.

CITY   STATE   ZIP

7 7 7	**WORTH FOUR FREE BOOKS PLUS A FREE VICTORIAN PICTURE FRAME**
🍒 🍒 🍒	**WORTH THREE FREE BOOKS PLUS A FREE VICTORIAN PICTURE FRAME**
● ● ●	**WORTH THREE FREE BOOKS**
🔔 🔔 🍒	**WORTH TWO FREE BOOKS**

Offer limited to one per household and not valid to current Silhouette Romance™ subscribers. All orders subject to approval.

© 1990 HARLEQUIN ENTERPRISES LIMITED   **PRINTED IN U.S.A.**

THE SILHOUETTE READER SERVICE™: HERE'S HOW IT WORKS

Accepting free books places you under no obligation to buy anything. You may keep the books and gift and return the shipping statement marked "cancel." If you do not cancel, about a month later we will send you 6 additional novels, and bill you just $1.99 each plus 25¢ delivery and applicable sales tax, if any.* That's the complete price, and—compared to cover prices of $2.75 each—quite a bargain! You may cancel at any time, but if you choose to continue, every month we'll send you 6 more books, which you may either purchase at the discount price ... or return at our expense and cancel your subscription.

*Terms and prices subject to change without notice. Sales tax applicable in N.Y.

BUSINESS REPLY MAIL
FIRST CLASS MAIL   PERMIT NO. 717   BUFFALO, NY

POSTAGE WILL BE PAID BY ADDRESSEE

SILHOUETTE READER SERVICE
3010 WALDEN AVE
PO BOX 1867
BUFFALO NY 14240-9952

NO POSTAGE
NECESSARY
IF MAILED
IN THE
UNITED STATES

The audacity of that remark was second only to the thrill it produced. Even as she felt her cheeks heat, she fought the need to smile, to simper even, to *flirt*. Resisting the urge, she turned away and stomped toward the trunk, her shoes squishing with every step. "My legs have nothing to do with it," she told him sternly, secretly pleased that he kept step with her, the umbrella framing them with cheery yellow and green.

"All right," he said congenially. "We'll chalk it up to the weather, then."

"Chalk what up to the weather?" she asked, turning the key in the lock of the trunk.

The trunk lid sprang up, scraping against the tips of Bolton's umbrella. He shifted position to keep from scratching the paint and said gently, "Your snappish mood."

She rounded on him. "I beg your pardon! I am not—" But she was, and there was no denying it. And yet he was smiling at her in a soft, intimate way that made her heartbeat speed up noticeably and her irritation vanish like smoke on a breeze. "You're right," she amended apologetically. "I'm sorry."

"No apology necessary," he said. "I'm just glad you're here."

She nodded and busied herself at the car trunk, looking for the umbrella.

"Did Wallis give you a hard time about it?" he asked lightly.

"Yes," she told him, "but it doesn't matter. I can handle my father-in-law."

His smile was still in place when she looked up again, her closed umbrella in hand. "I didn't doubt it for a minute," he said softly, and it was exactly the right thing to say, exactly what she wanted to hear.

Exasperated more with herself than with him, she gave up to the smile that was tugging at her mouth. "I don't want to be late for Bible study," she said.

He reached out and closed the trunk lid, then took her keys from the lock and placed them in her hand. "We'll run," he said, sliding his arm around her waist. "Stay close now."

She stayed close, and when they stepped into the quiet bustle of the church, her heart was pounding with more than simple exertion. Much more. And for the first time, she saw the folly of even trying to deny it.

Chapter Six

The crack of the bat brought half the crowd to its feet, but the ball went straight into Trenton's glove as if running on a string. The batter hadn't got off home plate before the umpire yelled, "Out!"

Clarice plopped down upon the bleacher with satisfaction. The boy had an uncanny talent for the game. Everyone said he was going to be a lottery player, a kid so good he was considered an unreasonable advantage for any team. His name would go into a hat with the other lottery players and the team reps would all draw in turn, according to their placings at the end of this season, the weakest team going first. It was the only fair way to distribute the real talent. Bolton said such talent was rare. Seldomly were there enough lottery draws for every team to pick, so the best teams usually got left out. Trenton said he didn't care which team he played on as long as he played.

He loved the game. He was kind of low-key about it, but it was obvious just the same. He never missed a practice,

never complained about the heat or the workouts or the dirt
and skinned shins from sliding into home. He never had to
be told to put up his gear, never had to be reminded to clean
and oil his glove. He was getting calluses on his catching
hand, calluses put there by the glove and the repeated
pounding of a ball into it. She had seen him swing a bat until he was so tired he could barely lift his arms, but he'd no
more have dreamed of giving it up than he'd have dreamed
of giving up breathing. Best of all, he never bragged, was
never overconfident or smug about his abilities. He accepted every word of praise calmly and quietly, then talked
of improving. Always, he talked of improving.

Being in the company of such talent was awesome and a
little frightening. One could see the possibilities stretching
out over the years to come and all the many things that
could put an end to them. An injury, unscrupulous coaches
or managers, the envy and resentment of friends and teammates, too much pressure too soon, disenchantment, burn-
out... Any or all could put an end to what might be a
brilliant career. She had to make the right decisions for him,
strike a balance between encouragement and support and
pushing. Bolton felt it, too. She could tell. Not too long ago
he'd discussed with her the wisdom of allowing Trenton to
play in a spring league.

"I don't know what's best," he'd admitted after telling
her of Trenton's desire to play in the early season. "On the
one hand, I wouldn't like to see anything keep him from
playing as long as it's what he wants, but I think he ought
to have the opportunity to experience other sports, too. He's
a champ at wrestling, a positive star at baseball. Why not
football and basketball, too, track and field, soccer? It's
occurred to me that he might have the eye, speed and disci-
pline for tennis, as well."

"Maybe we should just let him decide," she had suggested halfheartedly, but Bolton had shaken his head.

"He isn't even nine years old. He doesn't have the information or experience to make such decisions. He ought to be able to voice his preferences, but how can he know what he prefers if he doesn't experience or at least understand all the possibilities?" He had sighed then and rubbed the back of his neck with one hand. She'd been tempted to rub it for him but had kept her hands firmly in her lap until he'd stopped and spoken again. "On the other hand, it might be a mistake to let him spread himself too thin. Maybe he should be focused on a single goal. I just don't know."

"Well, neither do I," she had admitted blatantly.

That was when he had proposed that they get a little expert advice. "I know the athletic director at one of the state colleges. I'd be glad to talk to him, find out what he thinks."

It was that same named athletic director sitting on the bench next to Bolton this very evening. When Bolton had made that call, he'd been told that Carl Gallup was in Marlow visiting relatives. Marlow was a fifteen-minute drive from the baseball field in Duncan. Carl had insisted on taking a look for himself.

He was a likable man, friendly but rather intense, and bald as a billiard ball. Clarice didn't know why she found that so unappealing. More unappealing still were the speculative glances he kept moving back and forth between her and Bolton. Those looks had dwindled, though, once the game had started. Now every look he gave Bolton was filled with confirmation and, if she wasn't mistaken, a touch of awe. She could hardly wait to hear what he had to say about Trenton's abilities.

She didn't have to wait long. The game was in the bottom of the final inning when Trenton caught that straight drive. A few minutes later Trenton's team, the Tridents, added another number in the win column. Bolton and Carl stayed in the bleachers talking while the crowd thinned out and Clarice went to meet her son. Going for ice cream had quickly become routine for this team, and in honor of tonight's win, the coach was buying. Clarice gave her permission for Trenton to ride with the other boys in the coach's van but insisted first that he come up into the stands and meet Bolton's friend. He went along amiably, but the quickness of his step revealed his eagerness to be away. She didn't make him wait.

Once the introductions were done and both Bolton and Carl had praised the team's performance and then his own, Trenton reverted to the thought uppermost in his mind—a double-dip Rocky Road with sprinkles. "Will you and Mom come pick me up at the ice-cream shop, Bolt?" he asked, anxious to be gone.

Bolton smiled and tapped him on the forehead. "I'd like that." He looked a question at Clarice, and Trenton followed his lead. They did need to discuss Carl Gallup's advice.

"Sure," she decided aloud. "We'll be along in a few minutes."

Trenton smiled happily and went off after his friends. Clarice watched him go, wondering when was the last time she'd seen him so carefree. Maybe never.

"He's got the stuff all right," Carl said once the boy was out of earshot. "I've never seen better at his age. You say he's wrestling, too?" He went on at their nods. "Good training, but not my pick of sports for a boy with his abilities. Still and all, I'd let him do whatever he wanted to. My advice is to give him a taste of everything and let him decide where he wants to concentrate. More than likely he'll settle on one or two sports and lose interest in the rest. I'd say team sports definitely, if he's as even-natured as you portray him, but once he's settled, make sure he stays with it. Talent like that is too rare to let atrophy. If he stays with wrestling, Mrs. Revere, just make sure his coach keeps him in the proper weight class and doesn't starve him down to the next lower one. That's a favorite tactic with wrestling coaches, but it can slow a boy's growth if taken to extremes."

"I'll remember that," she promised. "Thank you so much for taking the time to talk with us."

"No problem," he said, getting to his feet. "I haven't had a chance to see the Bolt here since he played for me in college." He clapped Bolton on the shoulder. "That could be your kid there, old friend. He's got your kind of talent."

Bolton's eyes darted to Clarice when Carl said that, but she looked away, afraid her thoughts would show in her eyes. Bolton got up, too, and they all three climbed down the bleachers as if they were stairs.

"Would you care to join us for ice cream, Mr. Gallup?"

"No, thank you. I left family waiting in Marlow."

"How is your mother, Carl?" Bolton asked as they walked toward the parking lot.

"Hasn't aged a day in thirty years," Carl said. "Would you believe she's getting married again at her age? Neighbor fellow. I'm guessing he's eight to ten years younger than she is. More power to 'em, I say."

Bolton laughed. "I couldn't agree more. Give her my best wishes, won't you? And thanks again, Carl."

"Anytime."

The two men shook hands, and Carl went trudging off across the grass to his shiny new pickup truck. It was quite a vehicle, a yellow step-side, short-bed truck with his team's mascot stenciled on the doors and tailgate. Nobody would ever wonder about his loyalties. Clarice waited until he was a good distance away, then cocked an eye up at Bolton.

"The Bolt?" she queried succinctly.

Bolton grinned, for all the world as if he was embarrassed. He lifted a hand to scratch behind his ear. "It was kind of a nickname," he explained. "Athletes are fond of giving one another nicknames."

"Mmm-hmm, and just what did you do to get yourself that particular nickname?"

"A sportswriter tagged me with it," he said. "I think he wrote something about my reflexes being lightning quick."

"You think," she scoffed, enjoying his discomfort. "Mr. Gallup said something else that's got me wondering. He said Trenton has 'your kind of talent.' He was saying a lot, wasn't he? You really were very good."

He looked at her a long moment. "I told you I thought about going pro, had every intention of it, in fact."

"But when it came time..." she prompted.

He grinned. "You already know that when it came time to make the decision, I realized I wouldn't be happy anywhere but in the ministry."

"And no one tried to talk you out of that?" she asked gently.

He hitched up a shoulder. "Well, Carl did, of course, and Carol, too, briefly." He smiled wistfully. "She thought she was going to marry a million-dollar pro, you know, but once she understood how important the ministry was to me, she couldn't have been more supportive. She literally went to work and put me through seminary."

Clarice was surprised. "I didn't know." Somehow she'd never thought of a pastor's wife working outside the home. Either things had changed or Bolton Charles was a more extraordinary man than she'd realized—or both.

He nodded. "She was a schoolteacher, and a good one. She loved it, every minute of it. She worked until we came here. We intended to have children... Of course we never did." He looked away, but not before she glimpsed the pain in those dark eyes.

She wanted to touch him, to comfort him. She owed him that much. She laid a hand on his arm. "I'm sorry."

He turned back to her with a smile. "Me, too. Thanks."

She took her hand away, the flesh beneath it suddenly hot enough to scorch. "Trenton will be waiting. Want to take one car or two?"

"Let's take your car," he replied quickly, grinning, "and let's put the top down."

She laughed. "All right. Want to drive?"

"Oh, yeah. I thought I'd have to suggest it myself."

She laughed again, feeling light and young and somehow invulnerable. He had a way of making her feel that way and scaring her half to death all at the same time. She thought about what he'd said about wanting children, and she thought about what Carl Gallup had said, that Trenton could have been Bolton's son, and she thought about how, when Carl had said it, she had suddenly and fiercely wished it was so. Then it came to her that Bolton Charles had already been more father to her boy than his own father had had a chance to be. And like her son, she needed Bolton Charles. And that was the most frightening thing of all.

Bolton punched up the speed, grinning as the night wind whipped his hair about on his head, and Clarice sank lower into her seat, her hands clamped down over hers. An instant later he started slowing for the turn ahead, and she sat up straighter but didn't let go of her hair. *Miss Perfect,* he thought. *As if she wouldn't be beautiful if she were as bald as Carl.* He chuckled at himself. Only a man in love would think like that, and he was definitely a man in love, but apparently a man in love by himself. He couldn't resist a glance at her, in hope that something might have changed in the past ten seconds. It was a mistake. His heart, apparently, was sitting right up there in his eyes, and the instant she saw it, she panicked, her own eyes growing large and wild, like those of a hunted animal. He looked swiftly away, bemoaning his stupidity.

Why could he not stop pursuing her? She simply did not want him in that way. He knew she liked him, but that was the extent of her interest in him. Even a *hint* of anything more disturbed her greatly. He had prayed at length about this, requesting everything from wisdom to the strength to endure to a change of heart for each of them in turn. Through it all he had not been able to forget that persistence had won her for Trenton's father. But she was not a prize, for pity's sake! She was a person, a woman, a child of God with a heart and a soul and a mind and a life of her own, and if she was not meant for him ... The thought was a physical pain.

The silence beyond the whir of the wind seemed oppressively heavy. He reached down and flipped on the stereo. A tape was in the deck, and the night was instantly filled with the melodic strains of Tchaikovsky's *Nutcracker Suite*. The music seemed alive, growing, maturing. His spirits lifted. Pleasure filled him. He smiled to himself, wondering if this piece was a favorite of hers. He usually preferred the *1812 Overture* himself, and yet this was achingly sweet—and peaceful, so peaceful. He rolled his eyes heavenward in silent thanks and surveyed the star-filled velvet of the black sky. Automatically, he turned a smile on Clarice, wanting to share with her the pleasure of the moment. She visibly relaxed and laid her head back on the edge of the seat, dropping her hands. He concentrated on his driving, not daring to address the ache inside of him.

Had he not wanted to touch Carol this badly? Or was it simply that Carol had been so much more approachable?

Carol had loved him, after all. How he longed to be loved again. How he longed to be loved by Clarice Revere. He discovered that peace could be bittersweet.

They reached the ice-cream shop. He parked the car on the side of the road, glad to see that the small graveled parking lot was full. He was inordinately fond of the Gilleys. It pleased him that their little business was doing well. He hopped out of the car and hurried around to open the passenger door for Clarice. She was busily smoothing her hair. He resisted the urge to kiss her and tell her she was beautiful, waiting patiently until she was finished instead. She got out and smiled her thanks for his assistance. They walked across the street and entered the shop. Wyatt Gilley was wielding an ice cream scoop behind the freezer. He spotted them at once.

"Hey, Padre! About time you showed up!"

Bolton waved a hello. "How's Traci?"

"Still pregnant!" Wyatt declared happily. "Doc says she's got to stay off her feet more so the boys and I are holding down the fort for a while."

"Good for you. You'll let us know if we can do anything, won't you?"

"You bet." He turned back to the business at hand, a double-dip cone of Cherry Heaven. The "boys" were throwing pieces of waffle cone at one another and trying to catch them in their mouths. Bolton knew from experience how much help they would be. They were scamps, but he was as fond of them as he was of their father.

He and Clarice lined up behind a trio of others and began perusing the menu of flavors that hung over the freezer case. After a bit of quiet discussion, they each settled on a choice, Mocha Supreme in a cone for him, pineapple yogurt in a cup for her. Before Wyatt would take his order,

Bolton had to introduce him to Clarice and endure a bit of speculative eyebrow wiggling and thinly veiled teasing.

"Are you going to needle me or dip the ice cream?" he shot back finally.

Wyatt chuckled and addressed himself to Clarice. "I love to needle the Rev." He leaned forward conspiratorially. "Can't let him forget that I beat him out for the fair Traci."

Bolton rolled his eyes and felt heat spread upward from his chest. Now why should Wyatt's teasing suddenly embarrass him after all this time? Maybe it was Clarice's sharp glance. What nonsense! He searched his mind for a clever comeback but found none. He fixed Wyatt with a grim look. "Pineapple yogurt. In a cup."

Wyatt's grin puckered, but he bent his head and went to work. Bolton felt an intense urge to kick the man and was deeply grateful that the ice-cream freezer stood between them. He was acting like an idiot, and he knew it. When Wyatt handed him the cup, he passed it to Clarice. What was that in her gaze? It could *not* be accusation. He turned back to Wyatt and gave him his own order. The cone in his hand, he fished for his wallet.

"Oh, get out," Wyatt said gruffly. "Your money's no good here."

"Don't be silly."

"Out!" He punctuated the order with a smile of genuine fondness.

Bolton felt instant remorse and a welling of good feeling. "Thanks."

Wyatt waved him away and turned to the next customer. Bolton headed for the door to the deck, on the way in having spotted Trenton and his friends out there. At his elbow, Clarice spooned yogurt into her mouth and casually said, "Who is Traci?"

Bolton almost stumbled. He pulled the door open and looked down at her. "Traci is Wyatt's wife. She's expecting twins in a couple months."

"Oh." She trained her gaze on her cup and stepped outside.

Bolton followed, seeking to lighten the mood. "The amazing thing is," he said brightly, "they already have a set of twins, boys from Wyatt's first marriage."

"Two sets of twins!" she exclaimed. "My goodness, how will she ever manage?"

"Traci can manage anything," he said offhandedly. All at once, he felt a frisson of warning. He stopped wending his way through the tables and looked down at her. Her face was set, her eyes large and wounded. "What is it?"

She dropped her gaze to her yogurt. "You're in love with her, aren't you?"

He nearly dropped his cone. As it was, his jaw hit his chest. Was this jealousy? *Oh, God, please let this be jealousy!* He wanted to laugh, to throw his arms around her, lift her and swing her around and around in delight. He closed his mouth and swallowed. "Clarice," he said patiently, "it was nothing. I got them together. She's a dear young woman, a friend. I love her as I love all my friends, as I love Wyatt. Besides, I'm not the sort to carry a torch for a married woman."

Her eyelashes fluttered up. He saw regret in the green depths of her eyes. She smiled weakly. "It's just that you seem to be looking for someone, wanting someone."

"I am," he said tersely, and those big eyes grew bigger before the darkened lashes fluttered back down. He felt a sudden thrill of elation, a surge of hope. Was this the time? Should he speak now? She spooned yogurt into her mouth, her gaze targeted on her cup. A chair grated heavily across the planking of the deck. They were in public, for heaven's sake. What was wrong with him? He turned and led the way toward the table where Trent was laughing with his friends.

Greetings were exchanged. Chairs were pulled up. For some time, Bolton sat back and listened to the lively conversations of coaches, parents and eight-year-olds, while slowly working his way through the Mocha Supreme. Clarice was quiet, he noticed, but not Trent. The boy was bubbling in a way that Bolton had never seen before, and that gave him a great deal of satisfaction. Finally, the ice cream was all eaten and the celebration began breaking up. They walked through the shop to say goodbye to the Gilleys, then out onto the parking area and across the street toward the car. Some kid yelled a farewell to Trent, and Trent called back another, leaping up to add a wave to the parting. He had a friend. He was happy and carefree. Bolton's heart swelled with unmistakable parental love and pride. Whatever else happened—or did not happen—Trent was going to be all right, and he had had a part in that, however small. No regrets. He would have no regrets. That, too, was a gift.

He worked Clarice's keys from his pocket and held them up. She shook her head, oddly pensive since that exchange about Traci Gilley and his feelings for her. He clasped the keys firmly in his hand and opened the passenger door. Trent clambered into the back seat. Clarice slid into the front. Bolton closed the door and walked around to get in behind the steering wheel. He had something on his mind, something he'd wanted to ask all evening. He felt the time was right. He had prepared himself for a refusal. He had nothing to lose. Yet his hand shook slightly as he slid the key into the ignition. He changed his mind. Time remained. It need not be tonight.

Coward. Well, rejection was never pleasant. Might as well get it over with now, though.

Just then Trent stood up in the back seat and leaned forward. Casually he looped an arm around Bolton's neck and another around his mother's. "Coach says I'm getting strong," he declared, demonstrating with the tightening of his arms.

It was an excuse for a hug, nothing more. The pressure was significant but not painful, not even restrictive. Bolton smiled as he reached behind him to give a congratulatory pat on the boy's back. "Man, you sure are!"

Clarice turned and kissed Trent on the chin. To her evident surprise, the boy puckered right up and kissed her back. It was spontaneous affection and a measure of the boy's delight in the whole evening, perhaps even his life. Bolton held him tight with his awkward over-the-seat, behind-the-back hug. He loved this kid, could not love him more if he had planted him in his mother's womb and nurtured him every day of his life. Clarice lifted her gaze to his and held it there as if trying to tell him that she credited her son's happiness to him. He wanted so to pull her against him, to kiss her and then the boy, to laugh, to claim them as family. His family.

Yes, it was the time.

He slid his arms down, fixed a hand lightly over Trent's wrist where it lay against the base of his throat, and looked at Clarice. "We're having a special Independence Day celebration next week," he said. "Picnic on the grounds, games, recognition of our veterans, music and so on. Then afterward we'll all go over to the football field for the fireworks. I'd like you both to come and spend the afternoon with me."

His heart did not begin its pronounced painful beat until the words were said. He waited, one, two, three beats that rocked him against the seat. Clarice glanced at Trenton, who looked steadily, expectantly back at her, then she turned to Bolton and smiled.

"We'd love to," she said.

It took every ounce of his willpower not to gasp. His heart stopped and started over again with soft, rapid thuds that felt like a cloud expanding in his chest. Yes. Yes. Oh, yes. He closed his eyes briefly in thanks, then a got a hold on himself.

She had said yes to a picnic, nothing more. But it was a start, wasn't it? It was progress in the right direction. Now what? Where to from here?

One step at a time. One problem at a time. He heard Carol's voice once more admonishing him, slowing him, simplifying for him. He smiled and leaned forward, reaching for the key again. Clarice quietly insisted that Trent sit down and buckle his safety belt. The boy complied but not without first whining, "Oh, Mom!"

Clarice twisted around to glare at him, but then she blinked two or three times and turned to stare at Bolton. He knew exactly what she was thinking. Where was her solemn, careful, obedient little boy? The answer was obvious. Her painfully solemn, determinedly careful, unnaturally obedient little boy was turning into a real, genuine, actual kid. Bolton smiled and shrugged. She lifted a hand to her mouth and started to laugh. Soon they were both laughing, Trenton staring at them as if they'd lost their minds and asking uncertainly what was funny.

"It's not funny laughter," Bolton explained, starting the car on its way. "It's happy laughter, pal, happy laughter."

Trenton muttered something under his breath, something so *childlike,* so typical, that they laughed again. Bolton turned the corner and accelerated. A moment later, he glanced at Clarice. She was sitting upright in her seat, one leg curled beneath her, one arm resting along the rim of the window, the other draped over the seat. Her hands were nowhere near her head, and her hair was floating on the breeze. He laughed again, a purely private exercise.

God was so good, so very good. There truly would be no regrets. If this was the zenith, the best it could be, the sum of his relationship with these two special people, he could have no regrets. He hoped for more. He prayed for more. But if this was all the satisfaction he was ever to know, it was enough to hold regret at bay for a lifetime. He reveled in that, exulted in it. He had done some good where he had wanted to do good. Man could not ask for more than that, to spread a little bit of God over those he loved, for what was God if not everything good? He felt strengthened and empowered by the God he sought to serve, and for the millionth, billionth time, he felt his calling confirmed. It was enough—not all he wanted, but more than he deserved certainly. He filled his thoughts with these things, silently speaking them to the source of his satisfaction as he drove back the way they'd come.

The lights were off at the baseball field when he turned the car into the parking lot. The headlamps picked out stripes and chunks of gravel and cement markers and the sensible sedan he felt duty bound to drive. He stopped the saucy convertible directly behind the sedan and shut off the lights without killing the engine. He turned in the seat to tell Trent goodbye, only to find the boy slumped in exhausted slumber.

"He played awfully hard tonight," Clarice whispered in apology.

Bolton nodded and allowed his arm to stretch out along the back of the seat. "Yes. I wish you didn't have to wake him when you get home."

"He's too big for me to carry," she whispered wistfully.

"He's not too big for me," Bolton heard himself saying.

She looked away. "I know."

Pushing my luck, he thought, then chuckled. He didn't believe in luck. Faith guaranteed that everything happened for a reason. Still, he had been advised to take only one step at a time. He sighed and opened the door to get out. She did the same. They met at the front of the car. The engine rumbled softly, reminding them that time was short. He took her hand and squeezed it. "Good night, Clarice."

"Good night."

He released her and turned away, his footsteps scraping across the asphalt.

"Bolton?"

He stopped and slowly turned back. Had she changed her mind? Had she thought of a reason, an excuse to cancel out on the Fourth of July? *Oh, ye of little faith. Everything for a purpose.* She stepped closer in the dark.

"Could I bring something for the picnic? Fried chicken? Barbecued sausages? I used to cook, you know. I wouldn't mind."

He smiled at God. "That would be nice. It's potluck. Bring anything you want. Just be sure and tell me what it is. I wouldn't want to miss it."

"All right, then. Is there something you especially like?"

Something he especially liked. He savored that a moment, thinking. "Deviled eggs. Full of cholesterol and fat. I love 'em. I'm glad I don't know how to fix them for myself."

She giggled, sounding like a little girl. "The pastor loves deviled eggs. Wouldn't angel food cake be more appropriate?"

He chuckled. "I suppose so. I'd never thought of it that way."

"Nevertheless, deviled eggs you shall have."

"I look forward to it."

He felt her smiling at him. Then she turned and walked back to the car. She switched on the lights and pulled away. He watched until the car turned out into the street before taking his own keys from his pocket and heading home.

Everything for a purpose. One step at a time. He knew suddenly what that next step should be, and it gave the coming picnic special purpose. A special purpose with deviled eggs. He shook his head in wonder. Sometimes the blessings just came thick and heavy, overwhelming all the disappointment and confusion in a man's life. Sometimes going home alone was a little easier to bear, a little less lonely. Sometimes the promise was worth any risk, and love was once more a possibility. It was enough to make a man happy just to be alive, enough to make him thankful and humble and full of hope.

"Our Father who art in heaven," he began softly, "hallowed be Thy name..."

Chapter Seven

Bolton pushed half a deviled egg into his mouth, savored it as he rolled it around with his tongue and sighed. Only then did he begin to chew. Clarice shook her head, secretly thrilled—and openly worried.

"Are you sure you should keep eating those?"

He slid her a quelling look that the smile lurking at the corners of his mouth belied, then swallowed. "Are you sure that Teresa didn't make these?" he returned.

Clarice gave an outraged gasp. "Bolton Charles!"

He laughed, dark eyes crinkling at the corners. "It's just that these are so good, and Trent says Teresa is the best cook in the world. Maybe he just underestimates his mother."

"And maybe you just like to tease his mother," she accused.

He sobered and leaned back, hanging his elbows on the edge of the picnic table against which he leaned. "I do, you know," he said quietly, and the sound of his voice sent a shimmer of warmth through her. "You're very easy to tease. You take everything so seriously."

She looked away, narrowing her eyes at the tumble of boys sprawling and rolling on the grass. Trent had proudly announced that he was going to give a wrestling demonstration, and there had been much flipping and falling ever since. She hoped he wouldn't dehydrate in this hundred-degree-plus heat, not that it was so bad here in the shade. Despite her worry, what Bolton had said concerned her. She *was* too serious. Hers was not the only boy playing out there in the heat, and all the other mothers seemed content. Bolton would not keel over from a heart attack from eating a half-dozen deviled eggs, though he certainly shouldn't make a habit of such a thing, and it really wasn't any of her concern anyway. The look in Wallis's eye when she'd announced that she and Trenton were attending the Independence Day picnic had been murderous, but that didn't mean anybody was going to be murdered. She had agreed to attend this picnic at Bolton's behest and had even gone to the trouble of making his favorite food, but that did not mean that this was a date. Did it?

An older gentleman came up and challenged the pastor to a game of horseshoes. Bolton groaned dramatically as he got to his feet. "I'm full of deviled eggs, Seb. You'll probably beat me handily."

"I always beat you handily," the gentleman exclaimed good-naturedly, "and you're always full of devilment, whether it comes with eggs or not."

"Does this sound like respect to you?" Bolton asked Clarice rhetorically. "The minister is supposed to get a little respect."

Seb cackled. "I respect a man who throws a sound ringer," he said, thumping the pastor on the shoulder, "and a pretty woman. I sure enough respect a pretty woman."

Bolton smirked down at Clarice. "I guess you get all the respect then."

"She sure does," agreed Seb, giving her a wink.

Clarice laughed, absurdly pleased, especially when Bolton echoed Seb's wink with one of his own.

"Be back in a bit," he told her.

They ambled off to toss horseshoes at a stake. Not ten seconds later Trenton came running up. His face was flushed, and sweat had plastered his hair to his head. "Where's Bolt?" he gasped, reaching for a cup of lemonade.

"Playing horseshoes. Sit down and cool off." She snatched up a paper plate and started to fan him with it.

He dropped onto the bench. "Can I spend the night with Frankie Forrest this weekend?"

"I don't know. I'll talk to Andrea."

"She said it's okay."

"Then I guess it's okay with me, too."

"Neat." He swigged more lemonade. "Where did you say Bolt was?"

She stopped fanning. "Playing horseshoes. Why?"

"Think I'll go watch."

"You need to cool off."

"I'll cool off on the way," he insisted plaintively.

Clarice sighed. Sometimes lately she wished her "regular kid" was a little less "regular." Or was she being too serious again? Maybe a compromise was in order. "Well, if you really want to watch the horseshoe game, I'll go with you then."

He shrugged, glancing away, then rolled his eyes up at her. "Too late. The Gilleys are coming."

"Who?"

"The Gilleys. You know, from the ice cream shop, the ones with all the twins."

Clarice looked in the direction he indicated. Sure enough, Wyatt Gilley and a young woman with a swingy pony tail and an enormous stomach were moving slowly toward them. Clarice recognized her at once as the woman who had kissed Bolton's cheek on the sidewalk that rainy morning. Any hope she harbored that they meant to say a quick hello as they passed her by were dashed when Wyatt raised a hand and called out, "Clarice! I want you to meet my wife!"

Clarice got up and smiled, aware that Trent was trying to edge away from her. She caught his hand, stiffening her smile to keep it from slipping. "Hi."

"Hi." Wyatt's smile was open and friendly. "This is Traci. Well, most of it's Traci—the rest is baby." His pride rang in every word.

"Nice to meet you, Traci."

Traci smiled. "Thanks. You, too." She dropped her gaze to Trenton. "This must be the future all-star."

"My son, Trenton," Clarice said, noting that Bolton had obviously told the Gilleys all about her son, at least.

"Hi, Trenton."

"Hello."

"Maybe you've met our boys, a couple of redheaded outlaws named Max and Rex."

"Yes, ma'am."

"Well, try not to hold it against us," Wyatt quipped.

Traci poked him in the ribs with her elbow. "Wyatt!"

He laughed and folded an arm around her neck. "Just joking," he said to Clarice, who was aware that she was watching them too closely.

She couldn't help it. They were an unusual couple. Wyatt was older, harder, attractive in a macho way, while Traci was more than simply pretty. She had an innocence about her that was strangely compelling, a wholesomeness that certain men were bound to find irresistible. Dismayed, Clarice looked at the good skin, the pretty eyes, the lush mouth and the golden hair. Just as she'd feared, Traci Gilley was exactly the sort of young woman to incite devotion in a steady, domesticated male. Like Bolton. She wouldn't have put Wyatt Gilley in that category, but if the way he was looking at his wife was any indication—as if he could eat her bite by delicious bite—Wyatt Gilley's devotion was passionate to the point of indelicacy. For the third time, Clarice felt a sharp stab of envy where this woman was concerned.

Just then Wyatt said, "Where's Bolton?"

The question, which implied that she and Bolton would naturally be together, did much to soothe and perk up Clarice's feelings, yet unnerved her at the same time. She found herself stuttering. "Uh, h-horseshoes."

"And I want to go watch!" Trenton piped up.

Clarice glanced down into beseeching eyes. His face was no longer flushed, but a part of her still wanted to keep him near. Wyatt Gilley stepped into the fray.

"I'd like to go watch, too," he said. "Why don't we kind of amble over together?"

Trenton beamed, and turned those pleading eyes up at his mother again. She capitulated. "Oh, all right, but I expect you to *walk*. And drink your lemonade."

Trenton nodded eagerly, the cup already at his mouth. Wyatt smiled understanding at her, and he and the boy walked away. Clarice sighed.

Traci laughed. "They grow up too fast, don't they?"

Clarice nodded. "I guess you know that since you already have two boys."

Traci wrinkled her nose. "Actually, I only came on the scene about a year ago. Wyatt and his first wife were divorced and he eventually wound up with the boys." She slid her hands around her stomach, linking them underneath as if to help support the load.

"Why don't we sit down?" Clarice said, indicating the bench.

Traci sank down gratefully. "Thanks. I get tired awfully quick these days."

"I understand it's twins," Clarice said.

Traci laughed. "Yes, it is. Poor Wyatt. My grandmother says it's proof positive that God has a sense of humor. One set of twins is mayhem, two sets is just plain ridiculous."

"*Two* sets of twins," Clarice mused, shaking her head. "You don't look terrified."

Traci laughed. "Maybe I ought to be, considering Max and Rex. What those two can't get up to hasn't been invented yet. But, I don't know, I've loved the scamps almost from the start. Truthfully, it was Wyatt who terrified me."

Clarice cocked her head. "How so?"

Traci's smile seemed almost too private to share. After a moment, she shrugged. "He made me . . . *nervous.*"

"Oh?" Clarice's eyes grew round. Bolton made her *nervous* sometimes.

Traci leaned back, hands clasped over her stomach. "Well, he made me nervous and he didn't, you know? I mean, being with him always felt right, but he's not exactly a comfortable kind of man—like Bolton."

Like Bolton? Clarice thought. "I wouldn't really describe Bolton as 'comfortable.'"

"No?" Traci seemed genuinely surprised. "Huh, I always thought Bolton was the world's easiest man to be around."

Clarice was shocked. "You can't mean that. Why, Bolton Charles is the most *disturbing* man *I* have ever known."

"Oh?" Traci studied her for a moment, then grinned. "Oh."

Clarice was profoundly puzzled. "What?"

Traci slid a companionable arm around her shoulders. "Bolton is a terribly handsome man. I can see how he would *disturb* the right woman." Clarice felt her face blanch. Traci seemed amused. "Don't worry," she said, giving Clarice's shoulders a squeeze, "it's quite mutual. To tell you the truth, that's why I wanted to meet you."

"It is?"

"Certainly. Bolton's such a special man," she said, "that any woman he cares deeply about is bound to be special, too."

Clarice was stunned. Deeply? Bolton cared *deeply* about her? Suddenly she felt a sharp, intense yearning. Deeply. Instinct told her that having Bolton Charles care *deeply* about her could be the most exciting, the most thrilling, thing that had ever happened to her. She thought of the way Wyatt had looked at Traci, and she thought of Trenton's father. He had occasionally looked at her with that kind of hunger in his eyes, but she had always wondered if he was seeing her or somebody he was determined to turn her into. It wouldn't be like that with Bolton. Somehow she knew it wouldn't, and a part of her rejoiced while another recoiled in terror. Independence, she reminded herself. She wanted her independence. Didn't she? Suddenly she became aware that Traci was looking at her very strangely. She made herself smile.

"Would you like some lemonade?"

"Great! Thank you."

They were still sipping from their cups when Wyatt and Bolton came back from the horseshoe-tossing contest. "Did you win?" she asked gaily, aware that her pulse had sped up at the sight of him.

He grinned. "Seb will never forgive me."

She laughed. "Congratulations."

Wyatt sat down next to his wife and gave her a hammer-lock hug. Clarice supposed he really couldn't get his arms around her middle anymore, but that didn't seem to matter one whit to him. Bolton sat down next to Clarice and casually dropped his hand onto her knee. She had never been so aware of a hand in her life. It was hot and heavy and possessive, and she couldn't even breathe until he took it away, then she reached for a glass of lemonade. She squirmed. She couldn't help it. He made her so... nervous. She gulped, trying to steady herself, and asked after Trenton.

"He's eating watermelon with Max and Rex."

"Uh-oh," Traci said.

"We made all three take their shirts off," Wyatt said.

"Andrea Forrest is keeping an eye on them," Bolton added.

That was good enough for Clarice. "Well, I don't suppose they can get into any real trouble, then."

Traci lifted her eyebrows doubtfully but said nothing.

Bolton slipped an arm around Clarice's shoulders reassuringly. "Trent will be fine," he said softly against her ear. She shivered. It was a delicious feeling. He tightened his arm. Disturbing. Very disturbing. She swallowed lemonade and made herself sit calmly while Bolton, Wyatt and Traci made conversation.

Trenton showed up after a while, head, torso, arms and hands freshly washed. His shirt flapped from his back pocket. He plunked down on Bolton's knee and leaned back against his chest as if he belonged there. "Max put a watermelon seed in my ear," he announced. Traci shook her head. "But Mrs. Forrest got it out." He sighed and laid his head on Bolton's shoulder. "I'm stuffed. I think I need to go to sleep." Trenton closed his eyes. Bolton wrapped his arm around the boy's waist and picked up the conversation where it had left off.

Clarice wondered if anyone else had noticed how naturally the two of them seemed to gravitate to one another, how competent Bolton was with the boy. A glance at Traci and Wyatt, who were sharing a knowing, pleased look, told her that they had.

It was not yet dusk when Bolton roused the boy, but the picnic was thinning out, and the Gilleys, whose company Clarice had very much enjoyed, had gone in search of their two sons. They wanted to get to the stadium early enough to get a good seat, and they offered to save spots for Clarice and Trenton. Bolton was scheduled to give the invocation, so a seat would be provided for him on the sidelines. Meanwhile, the cleanup and ordering of the church grounds had begun.

Fully dressed again and refreshed by his nap, Trenton joined a large, rowdy group of kids picking up small pieces of trash, while Bolton went to make certain that the portable tables and benches were being properly stored away. Overcoming a sudden bout of shyness, Clarice determinedly joined a group of women making sure that any leftover food was properly stored or disposed of. The experience was a revelation of sorts. Having attended church regularly for a few weeks, she knew many if not most of the people attending the picnic, but even those she didn't know seemed to know her. Everyone, it seemed, had noticed that the pastor was "keeping company," and everyone was curious. Andrea Forrest admitted that she had fielded questions all day long but declared that everyone was pleased as punch that the pastor seemed to finally be settling on another woman.

"When Carol died," Andrea divulged softly, "we all worried so for him. Oh, how he loved that woman! But that's just the kind of man he is, you know, the kind to love a woman body and soul. We're all just so glad he's found someone else.''

Clarice was stunned and then dismayed to be considered Bolton Charles's "someone else." Her hopes that Andrea's answers would be enough to satisfy the curious, however, were quickly dashed. His church membership seemed to believe that anyone for whom Bolton Charles showed even casual regard would just naturally welcome any question they chose to ask. She was appalled to be queried on everything from her age to her health! At first, she had trouble maintaining a civil composure, but gradually she realized what was behind the questions. Bolton was greatly loved by these people. They wanted only the best for him, and they expected to take into their midst and love his "someone else." Anyone in whom he showed interest would naturally be of interest to them.

Their reactions to today's public pairing was understandable but troubling, and what troubled her most was how easily everyone accepted the idea of her and Bolton together. It seemed a fait accompli in the eyes of the church membership. Even Andrea said she had known from the beginning, whenever that was, that Clarice and Bolton were bound to get together. It did Clarice no good whatsoever to insist that she and Bolton were simply friends. One woman whom Clarice told this gave her a very knowing look and said, "Just friends, *now* maybe."

It seemed that everyone was intent upon making a romance from this, and after a while, considering the lovely day they'd had, Clarice had to wonder if maybe everyone wasn't on to something. Maybe she and Bolton were "right" for each other. Maybe they were supposed to be together. And maybe the whole bunch of them were jumping to absurd conclusions! *She* certainly didn't know what to think anymore. How could she when her own experience with love was so dismal? The idea that her husband had loved her "body and soul" was absurd in the extreme. In fact, he had seemed to like her best when she'd stayed out of the way and kept her mouth shut. It had been pretty obvious from the beginning that he had married her not because of a consuming love for her but because she fitted his list of qualifications for wife so well. God knew she had been quiet and biddable in the beginning, too needy to question, but it hadn't lasted, and Trent hadn't been able to hide his disappointment. Was Bolton thinking as Trent had? Did he believe that she would "fill the bill" as a pastor's wife?

He had made his romantic intentions obvious at first, but then she had voiced her misgivings and he had promptly promised her friendship, which he had unarguably delivered. Maybe that was what he wanted now. Maybe he had loved his Carol as intensely as everyone said, and maybe she was the only woman he could love that way. That made a certain kind of sense to Clarice. His attentions to her during the picnic, while pronounced, had been extremely casual, so much so that she couldn't quite conceive that he had found their every physical contact as electric and compelling as she had. If Bolton was looking at her in the same way that her late husband had, then that and everything to date made sense. He had even asked how Trent had won her! And come to think of it, his approach had even been similar. Like Trenton, Sr., Bolton had tried to sweep her off her feet, but then when she had proved less biddable than he'd assumed, he had backed off. Chances were Trent would have done the same thing if she'd only had sense enough to exert herself. Unfortunately, she hadn't known what she'd wanted then, and after her parents had died in that car crash, she really hadn't seemed to have any option other than to marry Trent Revere.

Well, she was no longer that timid, uncertain girl. She knew what she wanted. She wanted her independence, not some romantic ideal of love—as if such a thing even existed! But it had existed for Carol Charles apparently, and for an instant, Clarice felt an extreme, intense envy of that woman. Envious of a dead woman. How low she had sunk, to envy a dead woman! What was wrong with her that she could feel such things?

All right, independence was uppermost in her mind, but it wasn't as if she wouldn't *like* to be deeply loved. Everyone wanted to be loved, after all. But was she so desperate that she even envied the dead what they had left behind? Some things, she reminded herself sternly, were more important than love, such as having the means and the strength to care for oneself and one's son, to do what was necessary for the well-being of the family unit. Bolton Charles was necessary for Trenton's well-being. Therefore, he was necessary for the well-being of the family unit. The fact that she was the other part of that family unit was irrelevant. The fact that Bolton made her think of being kissed and caressed and cherished was also irrelevant, and she had known it all along. But this was the first time that knowledge had made her feel so sad.

Once the cleanup—and the questions—were done, Clarice tried to get into the spirit of the holiday again, but her thoughts had left her unaccountably sensitive, so she was a little hurt when Bolton suggested that they take separate cars to the fireworks show. It would be late afterward and because of his part in the program, he could be one of the last to leave. He didn't want to keep her and Trent out later than necessary as Trent seemed worn out by the heat and the hectic activity. His reasoning was sound, of course, even considerate, but he seemed preoccupied and more distant than at any other time all day, and she couldn't quite deny

her disappointment. Had Trenton been less enthusiastic
about the fireworks display, she might even have gone on
home and skipped the whole thing, but as it was, she had
little choice. She drove herself and her son to the football
stadium.

The Gilleys had acquired seats on the fifty-yard line about
five rows up into the bleachers so that they could see over
those who walked by in front of them. Wyatt had had sense
enough to bring the umbrella from the car and provide
shade for his pregnant wife, who was sipping from a tall,
lidded tumbler with a big, fat corrugated straw planted in
the middle. No sooner had Clarice taken a seat beside her,
however, than Traci got to her feet and put a hand to the
small of her back, saying she had to visit the ladies' room yet
again. With twins, she said, one seemed to have to go twice
as much. At this point, after a lengthy pause, Clarice realized that Traci wanted her to walk with her. She was glad to
do so, of course, but not particularly pleased when, once
they'd left the growing crowd behind, Traci asked point-
blank, "What's wrong?"

Clarice was taken aback. Was she so obvious that even a
woman who had known her only hours could read her like
a book? She momentarily considered running a bluff, then
decided against it. Traci Gilley was much too observant for
that. But how much should she tell Traci? Clarice took a
deep breath, sorting her thoughts. "It's just happening so
fast. Everyone seems to have paired me up with the preacher
just because we ate together at the picnic."

Traci smiled guilelessly. "You did a little more than just
take food together, Clarice. He was obviously waiting for
you when you arrived, and the rest of the day you two
hardly got out of arm's reach. Then there's Trent. Bolton
hasn't shut up about that boy in weeks, and somewhere in
the conversation there's always a reference to that wonder-

ful mother, the fine woman, the dear friend, the very taste-
ful, the very elegant Widow Revere. What are people
supposed to think?''

Clarice was more concerned with what *she* was supposed
to think. Those were all very pretty terms that had been ap-
plied to her, but were they Bolton's terms? She slid a glance
at her friend. "Has Bolton really said those things about
me?''

Traci gave her a direct look, her brows rising expres-
sively. "Oh, yes, among others, and I don't think Wyatt and
I are the only ones he's said them to.''

That was pleasing—unless... Clarice bit her lip, bucked
up her courage and asked, "What was his wife like?''

Traci shot her a surprised glance, but then returned a
calm, thoughtful answer. "I didn't know her, but I've been
told that she was tall and rather thin—and blond.''

Clarice grimaced, but then one shared characteristic out
of three was hardly sufficient to pronounce herself a carbon copy of Carol Charles. She needed more information.
"Is that all you can tell me?''

Traci shrugged. "Well, let's see. I've heard it said that she
was very supportive of her husband but that she didn't
mince words when she disagreed with him, either. I gather
she was likable and intelligent and quite strong, considering the selfless way in which she handled her illness. Certainly those who knew her had a great deal of respect for
her.'' She slid a knowing gaze at Clarice. "But I've never
heard her described as elegant, and Bolton has never sat in
my living room and gotten that smoky look in his eye while
describing her as a 'sensitive, sultry female.' He was talking
about you when he said that.''

A sensitive, sultry female? Sultry? Her? Traci reached out
and tugged at her sleeve. Only then did Clarice realize she
was standing still with her mouth hanging open. She clapped

it shut and starting walking again, silently digesting this new information. All right, so she wasn't Carol Charles made over again, but what significance that had, she didn't know. She asked no more questions, and Traci wisely refrained from giving her any unrequested answers. On the walk back to the bleachers, they traded relieved comments about the setting of the sun. Now maybe it would cool off.

Clarice had a hard time keeping her thoughts on the weather, though. Someone was playing patriotic music over the address system, but Clarice couldn't make herself pay attention to it. Likewise, she ignored the rambunctious identical redheads who were taking up space on the other side of Trenton, even though Wyatt leaned across her and Traci twice to admonish them. Clarice was not even cognizant of the presentation of flags by a local Boy Scout troop until Trenton tugged her to her feet to recite the Pledge of Allegiance. And then Bolton walked to the microphone standing forlornly in the center of the field and politely requested silence so that he might pray. Clarice's thoughts suddenly coalesced and focused on the sound of his voice, and she closed her eyes, feeling herself lifted into the presence of a great and generous God. Silently, against the background of Bolton's eloquent words, she petitioned for wisdom and understanding. It struck her how pleased Bolton would be with that course of action, and she smiled despite the confusion fluttering in her breast.

Thereafter, she was better able to concentrate on the program, to appreciate the synchronized drills of the marching unit sent from Ft. Sill, the salutes given the flag by the local National Guard squad, the homage paid local veterans. She was even able to pay attention to the blatantly political speeches delivered by certain public servants. The day had finally faded into pure night, bringing cooler temperatures and a kind of anticipation of the spectacle to come. The lights were turned off in the stadium, and the capacity crowd fell into silence, and then a soft *whump* signaled the launching of the first rocket. That was when someone stepped on her feet. *One of the Gilley boys,* she thought, twisting sideways. The rocket exploded with a loud pop, and gold specks of light in a waterfall formation filled the sky, but she saw only Bolton staring down at her apologetically, Bolton settling at her side and lifting Trent onto his knee, Bolton sliding his arm through hers and folding her hand in his. Bolton. Oh, Bolton. She wanted to put her arms about his neck and bury her face in the hollow of his shoulder. Instead she clasped his hand and turned her face to the sky, oohing and aahing with the rest of them, knowing that the fireworks between them, should they ever truly come together, would far surpass anything devised by man.

At about eleven o'clock, it was all over, and a satisfied throng was filing out of the stadium. The Gilleys elected to sit awhile and let the crowd thin out to spare Traci any more time on her feet than absolutely necessary. Clarice and Bolton by silent agreement stayed with them. Before long, Trenton curled up in Bolton's arms and went to sleep. When it was deemed time to go, Bolton insisted on carrying him out to the car, though he was far too big to be carried such a distance. The going was slow, owing to the weight of the boy in Bolton's arms and the advancement of Traci's pregnancy, but Clarice enjoyed the late-night atmosphere among friends.

They left the Gilleys at their battered old station wagon. Even the twins were subdued and yawning as they clambered inside, but Clarice had never felt so alive, so *charged.* After helping Bolton strap Trenton into the front seat, putting the seat back and watching her son squirm into a comfortable position for sleep, she reluctantly withdrew to take her leave. To her surprise, though, Bolton forestalled her. Catching her hand again, he pulled her toward the front of the car and turned to face her.

"I know I said I wouldn't press," he told her softly, "but I can't help hoping..." He stopped and lifted his hands to her shoulders. "Do you think you might just go out with me? The two of us, I mean, alone. We could have dinner. Everyone says that Italian place downtown is very good."

She was about to tell him that she would be pleased to have dinner with him when he suddenly lifted a hand to her throat and with thumb and pinky laid alongside the curves of her jaw tilted her head back.

"I want to kiss you so very much," he whispered. "I've wanted to all day, and I've kept telling myself that I shouldn't, that I couldn't, that you wouldn't allow it, but I still want to."

Clarice swallowed, feeling the strength and the heat of his hand and the incredible burgeoning of desire. Every part of her seemed to strain toward him, and she lifted her hands to his arm, waiting, wanting. His gaze fastened on her mouth. His hand tightened gently. His arm folded at the elbow as he brought her toward him. But then he stopped, dropped his hand and backed away, tossing careful glances around them. They were not alone. The parking lot was crawling with people still. She didn't care. She was shocked that she didn't care, by how much she wanted him to want her. She still held him by the forearm, her fingers curled against his firm, tanned flesh and caressed by a dusting of crisp black hairs. He looked down at her hands grasping him and covered them with his free one. His thumb ran over her knuckles lightly, possessively.

"Friday," he said, his voice husky and urgent. "Will you let me take you to dinner?"

She nodded. "Yes."

He gave a long sigh of relief. "Good. Good." His hand tightened over her hands on his arm. "I'd better let you go before we make a spectacle of ourselves."

He meant she had better let him go. With an act of will, she loosened her hold on him and let her hands slide away. He grinned at her, and she bowed her head, feeling herself blush. He cupped her chin and pushed her head up again.

"I take it this means you've changed your mind."

She didn't pretend not to know what he was talking about. "I guess I must have."

"I'm glad. I'm so glad."

She smiled weakly and bit her lip, vacillating again, frightened again. She had best go before she made a fool of herself. She turned away. "Good night, Bolton."

"Good night." He put his hands to his waist and watched as she took her keys from her pocket and got into the car. He stepped forward just as she reached to pull the door closed and caught the handle with his hand. "Friday," he said sternly, as if warning her that he would not be put off if she should change her mind. "We have a date Friday."

A date. How many years had it been since she had gone on a date? How many years since she had wanted to? She did want to, and she was going to. Smiling up at him, she said, "Friday. I look forward to it."

Beaming, he closed the door and left her.

Chapter Eight

Wallis fixed her with a fiery look, his green eyes glowing almost eerily, their color oddly vibrant in his long, pasty face. "I forbid it," he said, his voice flat, implacable.

Clarice almost smiled. It was exactly what she had expected. Everything about this moment was exactly what she had expected from Wallis Revere. He still could not fathom that she might challenge—no, *deny*—his authority over her. His will had always proven supreme, even when her husband had lived, or perhaps *especially* when her husband had lived. Wallis could not be blamed if he did not comprehend that she had changed, for she had not fully realized it herself until now. How ironic that she should feel so strong, so sure, so sympathetic now. She had not expected that, especially not the sympathy, and yet he made such a sad picture sitting there in that chair, his body withered and gnarled and old, his spirit undiminished but ineffective for once. She bowed her head, sympathy softening her tone but affecting her resolve not at all.

"I'm afraid you have nothing to say about it, Wallis. He will be here any moment now, and I will be going out to dinner with him."

Disbelief and then anger twisted the old man's face. "How can you? How can you? He was for Trenton! What kind of mother are you?"

This time she did smile but sadly. "A good one, I think. A better one, at any rate, than I have been before."

"It's preposterous! It's unforgivable! You betray your son in this, and I'll be very sure he knows it! Think of that."

She shook her head. "What nonsense. There is nothing preposterous or unforgivable about a dinner date with a friend of my son's, a very much older friend, and you won't convince Trenton that there is. I think he was quite pleased when I explained it to him."

"Pleased? *Pleased?*" Wallis shouted. "How can he be pleased when you betray the memory of his father with the very man chosen to help him be *like* his father?"

Her mouth dropped open, then curved upward with a laugh, a single syllable that conveyed both her astonishment and her disdain for her father-in-law's peculiar view of the matter. He stiffened at her reaction, confusion warring with anger in those emerald eyes. She covered her mouth with her hand, stifling any further sound until she was well in control. She stepped closer, entreating him.

"Wallis, surely you understand that Trenton has no real memory of his father."

A look of pain flitted across the long, proud face. He worked his jaw side to side and set it. "You'd like to think that, wouldn't you?" he accused.

Shocked, she rocked back on her heels, but only the sounds of the words were shocking. The words themselves, the idea they conveyed, struck her with dismaying familiarity, though she had never acknowledged them before. It was true. She did not want Trenton to remember his father, not as she remembered him: selfish, self-centered, spoiled, arrogant, the bully who could not stand up to his father, alternately charming and angry and ultimately cruel with his complete lack of love for anyone or anything other than himself. It was true, and it was false, because she did not want it to be that way. She wished with all her heart that Trenton could remember a loving, giving, wise father whose first priority had been the well-being of his family. *A father such as Bolton Charles would be.* The thought came unbidden to her mind, more shocking than anything before it but utterly inevitable. She pushed it away, grasping instead at her father-in-law's anger and the facts surrounding it.

"You're being foolish, Wallis," she said sharply. "Trenton was barely three when his father died. That can't be changed. Most importantly, no one can make Trenton be like anyone but himself, and no one has a right to try, but the very last person who would is Bolton Charles."

A smirk twisted his mouth. "I never thought he would."

She cocked her head. "Didn't you?" Those emerald eyes sparked, narrowed. A shiver ran down her spine. "What do you mean? What *do* you expect of Bolton?"

He would not answer her. She saw it in the pursing of his lips even before the doorbell rang, but by then it was too late anyway. Bolton was coming. To her dismay, Wallis lifted his chin, composed himself. She felt a moment of panic, of unreasoning fear. No, she would not let him frighten her. She would not be defeated any longer by the fear of what could be. She pressed her hands together as she pushed at that fear, pummeled it and subdued it finally when Teresa's familiar face appeared around the edge of the opened door.

"Meester Rev'rend Charles," the maid announced cheerily.

Clarice opened her mouth to say that she would be right there, but Wallis snatched the opportunity from her.

"Show him in, Teresa."

Clarice shot him a wary glance, but his own gaze was targeted on that door, through which Bolton suddenly stepped.

"Wallis. Clarice." His smile was warm, relaxed, but the look he slid over her announced that he was prepared for anything Wallis chose to throw at him. He turned his attention to the old man. "I hope you're feeling well."

Wallis waved away his concern with a lift of his hand. "We'll have to talk soon," the old man announced. "Determine a convenient time and leave a message with Teresa. I'll look forward to it."

Bolton's mouth quirked, but he inclined his head and smoothly agreed before turning his gaze upon Clarice again. He smiled. "Ready?"

She nodded, wondering suddenly if this was not a mistake after all. He slipped an arm around her, his hand lying lightly against the small of her back, and turned her toward the door. Warmth suffused her. Warmth and ease. They stepped out into the hall and walked side by side to the foyer. There Bolton hurried ahead to open the door for her.

"You look very lovely," he said softly as he pulled the door closed behind them, "but then you always do."

She heard herself laughing, and wondered from whom she had borrowed that gay, musical sound. Surely she had never sounded like that before.

He took her hand and led her toward his sensible sedan. "Was Wallis being difficult?"

"No more than usual, I suppose."

"He did not like the idea of the two of us going out, did he?"

She shook her head. "But he would not like the idea of me going out with anyone."

He smiled down at her. "Yes, I know."

"Do you? How?"

"I've known people like Wallis before. To them, love is power, and power is used to control, so if they love someone, they must control them. It's the only pleasure they ever derive from love, but of course it is self-defeating. Controlling someone, or attempting to, is the surest way to lose them. That's why being a parent is so very difficult at times. One must constantly walk that fine line between responsible guidance and outright control. Sometimes our children shove us right over the line themselves, and then we have to have the courage to do what is best for them even if it means losing their love for a time. Between adults, however, control should never be an issue. Mature love of all kinds thrives best in an atmosphere of trust and respect and confidence. All of which means that Wallis Revere has never experienced a mature love, and therefore I pity him. End of sermon."

She stood there looking up at him for a long moment, marveling at his insight and the lucidity of his arguments, making it her own. *Between adults, control should never be an issue, for love thrives best in an atmosphere of trust and respect and confidence.* Wasn't that what she had been calling independence? She couldn't be sure. Her mind seemed to be saying one thing and her heart another, and all the while her body was clamoring nervously at Bolton's nearness. She realized suddenly that he was looking intently at her mouth, and her every cell seemed to focus on his. She forgot the sermon, forgot dinner, forgot Wallis. Suddenly Bolton stepped back, cleared his throat and reached for the car door.

She was not, it seemed, going to be kissed, and though before his kiss had frightened her, it now held a certain appeal. But would she have to tell him that? Could he not just kiss her when the opportunity presented itself? He had said that he wanted to, but perhaps he had changed his mind. Maybe it was best if he had. She couldn't decide. She no longer knew what was best where she and Bolton were concerned. Would she ever? she wondered. Did she even dare?

He watched her from the corner of his eye. She held herself so proudly, spine straight as a plank, shoulders leveled, her feet crossing in front of one another slightly as she walked with that graceful, swaying gait. High heels and a long, softly pleated skirt added to the effect, its muted jewel tones printed in paisleys and flowers, but it was the body-hugging lilac-colored sweater with its airy knitted pattern, short sleeves and wide neckline almost baring her shoulders that drew his eye time and time again.

He had not realized her dainty figure was also so lush. Her collarbone stood out slightly, adding definition to the graceful joining of throat, shoulders, and chest and begging to be tasted with mouth and tongue. Lower, her chest blossomed into the full, firm mounds of her breasts then tapered abruptly to a waist so tiny that he could easily span it with his two hands, even given the wide, soft gray leather belt and heavy silver buckle that lapped it. Below that belt, her gently flared hips swayed and slender legs glided in an unbroken stride that carried her small feet lightly across the ground.

He could not seem to stop himself from touching her, but he knew he must be satisfied with placing a hand in the middle of her back. He had an excuse for that much, at least, while they crossed the street. Then, as she climbed up those two steep steps to the broad sidewalk, he could take her arm, one hand above her elbow, the other below, and as he stepped up beside her, one hand slipped down to cup her elbow. It seemed natural enough to keep it there as they walked side by side to the corner. When he opened the door onto the narrow spiral staircase that descended into the intimately darkened restaurant, he smiled, then took her hand and stepped down before her, leading her carefully around and down until they reached the carpeted floor below.

He let his hands settle about her waist as she stood in front of him, her back to his chest, while they looked around the room and waited for the hostess to reach them. Candles burned inside pierced earthenware pots on every table, most of which seemed set for two with crisp white-and-burgundy linens. Music played softly in the background. Bolton picked out the sounds of violin, accordion and tambourine blended into a flowing stream of rising and falling notes. Potted plants somehow flourished in the dim light. Brick and stucco and unpolished marble lent atmosphere, and a quietly tinkling fountain in one corner provided a focal point for colored lights, while aproned waiters moved silently between tables, heavily laden round trays balanced upon uplifted palms.

"Two?" the hostess, a tall, slender woman with dark hair and cheekbones so pronounced they gave her a gaunt look, asked. Bolton nodded. She extracted two menus bound in red leather from a stand beside the stairwell. "This way please." She pivoted and strode confidently through the maze of tables.

Bolton tightened his hands on Clarice's waist, ostensibly as a signal to follow the hostess. In reality, he just wanted to deepen his touch, to feel her flesh mold itself to his hands, but when she stepped forward, he released her, robbed of his excuse to touch, and followed behind. His eyes were on those slender shoulders to which her little sweater clung so lovingly, so he did not see the familiar faces until he was nearly past them and only then because a deep voice called his name.

"Bolton."

He stopped, reaching automatically for Clarice and finding the curve of her hip. Satisfied that she had halted her forward progress and was even then moving back to him, he looked down. "Rod!" A grin split Bolton's face as the big cowboy got lumberingly to his feet. He shot a hand out and felt it clasped as he bent to drop a kiss on the cheek of the woman seated at the table. "Layne, how are you? I haven't seen you two in a while."

The woman wrinkled her nose. "We're teething," she said. "Poor Neddy. You know how it is, fussing and achy gums and sniffles. We dumped the little darling on Sam and Dedra and escaped for an evening of peace and quiet."

"Heather loves to play with Cousin Ned," Rod explained. "She doesn't even seem to mind his gnawing and drooling, and of course Sam and Dee have been through it already with her."

"It must be nice to have someone you can trust to sit for you," Bolton said, drawing Clarice closer. "Let me introduce you to my date."

"We were hoping you would," Rod admitted, sliding a look at his wife before settling his frank gaze upon Clarice.

"Clarice Revere," Bolton said. "Rod and Layne Corley."

"Hello."

Layne smiled up at them. "Are you new to the area, Clarice? I don't think I've seen you before."

"Oh, no. I've lived in Duncan ever since I married. I just haven't gotten out much since my husband died."

"So sorry," Layne said. "I didn't mean to raise a painful subject."

"He died a long time ago," Clarice answered gently, and Bolton could not resist the urge to slip a protective arm about her waist. Rod snapped his fingers.

"Wallis Revere," he said. "You must be Trent's wife."

"Widow," Bolton corrected shortly, surprised at how much he disliked hearing her described as Trent Revere's wife.

"Yes, of course," Rod mumbled, telegraphing Layne an eloquent look. Clarice glanced down in embarrassment. Rod changed the subject adroitly. "This is a favorite place of ours. Food's good. Lots of ambience. This your first time here?"

"Yes." Clarice and Bolton spoke in unison.

"Ah," he said with apparent satisfaction, "then let me recommend the ravioli."

Layne raised a hand in protest. "The spinach tortellini," she pronounced, "and the house salad."

"Definitely the house salad," Rod concurred, "and the cheesecake."

"The Amaretto cheesecake."

Bolton laughed. "Sounds great! But we aren't getting any closer to it standing here."

"Why don't you join us?" Rod asked. "We haven't ordered yet, and—"

"Thanks," Bolton cut in smoothly, "but I don't think so, not tonight."

Layne grinned. "Special occasion?"

"Just a private one." Bolton moved his hand to the small of Clarice's back and gave her a gentle push.

"Nice to meet you," she said over her shoulder, gliding away.

Bolton winked and smiled, hard on her heels. "Well," he heard Layne say behind him, "what do you think of that?"

"About time," her husband replied drolly.

Amen! Bolton agreed in silence. He was sick of being alone and more than ready for a real relationship again. The careful steps leading to this first date had been fraught with tension and frustration and longing, and now that he finally had Clarice to himself for an evening, he had no intention of sharing her. Given the opportunity, he would gladly make it a habit.

The patient hostess guided them across the room to a table in the far corner. Bolton smiled his thanks as she handed him his menu. "Can I get you anything to drink?"

"Tea for me," Clarice said.

"And me."

"Your waiter will be Steve," the hostess informed them before departing.

They looked over the menu in silence until the hostess returned with their drinks and a basket of warm breadsticks, fragrant with yeast and butter. Clarice was the first to close her menu and set it aside.

"Made up your mind?" Bolton asked lightly.

"I like Layne's suggestion."

He smiled over the top of his menu. "So do I. Spinach tortellini then. What about the sauce?"

"Marinara."

"Ditto. House salad?"

"Of course."

He laid down his menu. "That was easy."

"The recommendation helped."

"Yes."

She looked down at her lap, then up again. "It must be awkward, going out in public when you're so well-known in town."

"Not really. I'm aware of the scrutiny, but it would only bother me, I think, if I was doing something shameful."

"And the Reverend Charles would never do anything shameful."

It was a statement of trust, and it went without saying that he would uphold it as a sacred responsibility.

"Not intentionally," he said, "but like everyone else's, my judgment falters on occasion."

"And when it does?"

He smiled. "Once I realize what I've done, I face God with it, accept His forgiveness and rejuvenation and start over."

"You make it sound so easy."

"The hard part is the first part, realizing that I'm at fault, but you kind of get the hang of it after a while, and that's when you realize how imperfect you really are."

She laughed. "I see your point."

He smiled at her, and an easy silence slipped over them. He was content just to sit and look at her, absorbing her with his eyes. The arrival of the waiter, while welcome, was nevertheless an intrusion. Bolton made quick work of the matter, ordering for both of them, then sat back to look at her some more. After some time, a faint stain began to glow upon her cheeks. It was very becoming, but he knew he was disconcerting her. He made a stab at small talk.

"The days are so long in summer. It was bright as noon at seven o'clock."

"Was it? I'm afraid I didn't notice."

"It won't really be dark before nine."

"And even then it won't be cool," she said helpfully.

"No, it won't be cool."

They seemed to have exhausted the subject, and he couldn't think of anything else to say. He was staring at her again. He forced his gaze away, focusing on a point just above her shoulder. How absurd that he couldn't just talk to her. He had always been able to talk to her, but somehow the stronger his feelings grew for her, the more afraid he was of saying or doing the wrong thing. And his feelings had grown very strong, very strong indeed. He wanted so desperately to make her his own, to have the privilege of watching her grow and change as a person. He wanted to be able to look back at some point in his life and see how she had changed him. He was eager for that change, knowing that she could only affect change in him for the better, as Carol had done in her way. He had believed with all his heart that Carol was the mate of his soul, the love of his life, and now he knew—much to his amazement—that the love he had felt for Carol had only increased his capacity for that emotion. He could have been happy with Carol for the rest of his life, but he knew now that he could have that with Clarice, too. But how many chances would he get? Did another woman exist in this world whom he could love as he loved Clarice Revere? He didn't believe so. His heart was so very full at this moment that he couldn't conceive of feeling more, of *bearing* more.

"What are you thinking?" Her voice, soft and silky and treasured, invaded his reverie. It was only his own reply that he heard with horror.

"How much I love you."

His eyes zipped back to her face. She looked stricken, the color drained from her cheeks, her mouth slightly ajar. Talk about faulty judgment! He restrained the hand he'd almost smacked against his forehead and groped for a way to undo it, but what now could he say without giving a lie to the bald truth? She actually recovered first, swallowing and blinking rapidly several times. She laid her hands on the table and leaned forward slightly.

"You can't mean that."

"I didn't mean to *say* it."

"Why did you?"

He took a chance, an enormous chance, and reached across the table to cover one of her hands with his. "Because it's what I feel. You caught me off guard, and I just blurted it out. I'm sorry."

She looked down at his hand covering hers and swallowed again. "How do you know?" she asked so quietly, he barely heard her.

He tried to order his thoughts. "Well, because I've been in love before, and all the signs are there. I can't stop thinking about you, and half of what I think could get my face slapped, frankly."

She actually smiled. "Probably." Suddenly she looked up, her face naked and deeply solemn. "Maybe not."

His breath caught, and his chest seemed to expand at the same time. He squeezed her hand convulsively, then made himself let it go. Suddenly he was speaking again. "I—It was so easy with Carol. No surprises, no doubts. We met, and gradually we drifted closer. I don't even remember who said it first. It just evolved into a fact. But with you..." He shook his head, searching for words to make her understand. "You were sitting in my office that first day, checking me out to make sure I'd be a good influence on your son, and then—I don't know why—you relaxed and smiled at me, and I felt like I'd been poleaxed! Every time I saw you after that, I wanted to whoop and laugh and swing you in circles, and at the same time, it was eating me alive. Does she like me? Could she accept me? Might she possibly— please, God!—care for me just a little?" He closed his eyes. "I knew, of course, right after I kissed you that it wasn't mutual, so I tried to be your friend." He opened his eyes, meeting hers unflinchingly. "I *am* your friend."

This time it was Clarice who reached across the table, taking his hand in both of hers. "I know, but—"

Genuine panic seized him for perhaps the first time in his adult life. "Don't say it! Not here, not like this. Wait until we can talk it through in private, *please.*"

She canted her head, looking at him oddly, and licked her lips as if stoking her courage. "I was going to say that maybe we ought to try that kiss again and see if you draw a different conclusion this time."

He straightened abruptly. Try that kiss again? Different conclusions? He skittered a gaze around the room, and sat back. She wanted to try that kiss again. He gulped to start his heart beating, and suddenly the waiter was at her elbow, bending to place an oval platter before her. She looked down at the green curls of pasta nestled in thick red marinara sauce and sprinkled with shredded Parmesan, and Bolton had an abrupt vision of lifting her face with his hands and fastening his mouth to hers. Thankfully, he was distracted by the waiter setting his own plate in front of him and quickly became aware of the need to breathe. He filled his lungs with a sharp intake of air. Clarice looked up at him, her delicate brows arched. His mouth quirked up at one corner.

"After that announcement, I suppose you expect me to actually get through dinner without choking?"

A grin crossed her mouth. "Don't worry. I'm familiar with the Heimlich maneuver."

A joke. She was joking with him, and he was touched, deeply, gratefully touched. "You never cease to amaze me," he told her softly.

She gave him a timid smile and picked up her fork. He managed to follow suit and somehow consume his dinner, though how he managed, he would never know. His hand moved and the food disappeared from his plate, but afterward he couldn't remember chewing or swallowing or even tasting the plump green "ears" of pasta. He was giddy as a schoolboy on the first day of summer vacation, and every ounce of his willpower was required not to get up, grab her by the hand and haul her off to the first dark corner he could find. He tried not to think about it, but he couldn't think of anything else. He couldn't glance at her without focusing on her mouth, without feeling his own tingle in longing. He tried silently reciting the names of the books of the Bible and lost his way somewhere around Jeremiah. He was utterly miserable and strangely elated, and his hands were shaking so badly that he was embarrassed. He was grateful beyond words when, sufficient pasta having disappeared from their plates to have done justice by their dinner, Clarice declined dessert and he was able to pay the check.

At long last, they were on their feet and moving. He studiously avoided so much as a glance in the direction of the Corleys' table, and so left without even knowing whether or not they remained in the building. He let Clarice go up the spiral staircase before him and scrupulously allowed his gaze to move no higher than the trim ankles that moved up and down below the hem of her skirt. At the top, she stepped aside, and he pushed open the door against a summer evening as silky and warm as a relaxing soak in a full bathtub. It was not dark, but the sun had gone and the shadows of dusk had lit the street lamps and softened the air. They had the street entirely to themselves.

Bolton reached out a hand but did not dare touch her, not yet. He couldn't trust himself, knowing what was coming. They walked down the sidewalk and stepped down to street level, crossing directly in front of the sedan. It was darker here, the light of the street lamp filtering down to them through the branches of a big old hickory growing at the edge of the graveled parking lot. Bolton escorted her to the passenger side of the car and opened the door. She turned and dropped down to the edge of the seat, ready to slide inside, and suddenly he couldn't let her. He couldn't bear another minute without having her in his arms, without tasting her mouth. He stepped forward and reached down to cup his hand beneath her elbow. Wordlessly, she looked up, then slowly rose and came into his arms.

He folded her close and bent his head, experimentally brushing his lips over hers. She pushed her arms beneath his and hooked her hands up over his shoulders. Going up on tiptoe, she pressed her mouth to his. Their lips molded and blended softly. A slow heat spread through him, flowing downward into his chest. He flattened his hands on her back, fitting her more exactly to his body, feeling the weight of her breasts against him. She moaned and adjusted the tilt of her head, opening her mouth for him and firing the blood that plunged to his groin. He turned her slightly and walked her backward two steps, pressing her against the car, but he couldn't bring her close enough, and delving his tongue into the sweet, wet chamber of her mouth only deepened and hardened his need. But he couldn't stop for a long while.

Finally, with the far-off murmur of voices, good sense returned and prevailed. He retracted his tongue and gently separated their mouths, loosening his embrace at the same time. He even managed to move his feet backward a few inches, but he kept his eyes closed until the last possible moment, holding on to the sensations and even then holding the memory. When he did open them, it was to the shadow-blurred vision of her face. She had never looked so achingly beautiful to him as she did in that moment. Her eyes were large and luminous with wonder, her cheeks flushed a rosy pink, her mouth soft and lush with the effects of his kiss. He closed his eyes again, fixing that vision within him for all time, and despite the fire that burned still in his blood, despite the ache of unassuaged need, despite the cries of his heart that went without answer, he knew the joy and peace of loving with every fiber of his being. He knew, too, that it was a blessing to love so, and whatever happened, he would always have that. Forever after, when he counted his personal blessings, he would always count this moment. He might even count it first. Yes, definitely first.

Chapter Nine

"**Y**ou've kept me waiting weeks."

"So I have, but you did say that I should choose a date and time convenient to me, and I'm a pretty busy fellow these days."

"Busy squiring my daughter-in-law around town."

Bolton smiled. Well, at least the old man was laying it on the line for a change. No obfuscation today. So much the better. But somebody should have told old Revere that even a minister could play hardball when necessary, especially *this* minister. Bolton crossed his legs and lounged back in the comfortable wing chair, every bit as at ease as he seemed. "I enjoy your daughter-in-law's company. And I intend to go right on enjoying it."

"At what price?" Wallis queried sweetly.

Bolton fixed him with a frank look. "Any."

The old man chuckled. "I think not. First of all, I'll refuse you permission to see the boy."

"Refuse away. You're not the boy's guardian, Clarice is."

"You have betrayed your calling," Wallis came back smoothly. "You have influenced the boy for ill and the mother for worse. He was a quiet, obedient boy before you came in."

"He was a repressed, sad child before I came in," Bolton corrected. "And now he's a normal one."

"I expected you to teach him respect for his elders!"

"He already had respect for his elders."

"No longer! He argues with both his mother and me at every turn!"

"No more so than any other normal kid."

"He's uncontrollable!"

"In a pig's eye. He's just not under your thumb anymore." Bolton sat forward, upper body weight propped on one elbow as he leaned into the arm of the chair. "Tell me something, Wallis. What exactly did you expect to happen when you brought me into this situation?"

"I expected you to exert a little manly influence on the boy, wean him away from his mother's apron strings."

"Ah." Bolton leaned back again, shaking his head. "You thought I would help you negate Clarice's influence on her own son."

The old man frowned and hunched his shoulders defensively. "No such thing. She coddles the boy, babies him."

"You want him firmly within your own orbit," Bolton went on doggedly. "But you're stuck in that wheelchair. It's a lot easier to separate a boy from his mother's influence when you can separate him from her physically, isn't it? That's what you needed me for. I was supposed to be your legs, wasn't I? I was supposed to keep him out of the house and occupied, except for those times when you wanted him here with you so you could fill his head with idiotic notions about loyalty to a dead father."

"How dare you! A boy should not forget his father! I've tried to keep his father alive for him!"

"You've tried to turn him into his father, but that wheelchair has kept you from repeating your past performance. You couldn't drag him around with you to see to it that he spent as little time as possible with his mother, and you couldn't keep his mother confined to this house, either. It helps a great deal if you can confine the little woman to the house, doesn't it?"

Bolton feared for a moment that he'd gone too far. The old man's face had gone white as death while a splotchy red crept up the reedy column of his throat. His gnarled hands clutched at his chest, and Bolton's first thought was that he was having a heart attack. But then that pale, lean face contorted, and Bolton knew that what he was looking at was the very countenance of rage.

"You've stolen my family away from me!" Wallis roared. "And you've done it by seduction! What kind of minister are you? No man of God tempts another man's wife into his bed!"

He had half expected this. "Don't be absurd."

"I've seen her after you were through with her!"

Bolton sprang up to his feet, as angry as he'd ever been. But knowing that a cool head would serve him far better than a caustic tongue, he tempered that anger with righteousness. Being in the right never hurt. "First of all, she is *not* another man's wife. She's a widow. Second, neither of us has done what you're inferring."

The sneer on Wallis's face was evil. "We'll see what your church members think about it."

"I think my credibility with the church members will far outweigh yours."

"With some of them," Wallis said slyly, "but not with all."

Bolton looked him square in the eye. "So be it."

"I'll ruin you."

"I don't think so, Wallis." Bolton turned and walked toward the door, his grasp on his temper tenuous. "You see, I haven't done anything wrong, and neither has Clarice. Oh, and one more thing..." He stopped and looked back over his shoulder. "I'm *not* through with her. I never have been, I'm never going to *be,* through with her." He walked to the door and opened it. "I love Clarice, and I have every intention of marrying her. Think about that, Revere, and remember who really calls the shots where your grandson is concerned."

Wallis's face went slack, but then those green eyes flashed malevolently and narrowed. "*I* call the shots, Preacher, as you'll soon discover."

Bolton thought it best not even to answer that. He went out and slammed the door. It wasn't the only thing he'd have liked to have slammed, but the ministry had its price, and he'd always been willing to pay it—God's price, thankfully, not Wallis Revere's. But he couldn't let Clarice or Trenton pay Wallis's price, either. He had to convince Clarice to marry him, and the sooner the better for all their sakes. Now if only he could do that. Oh, God, let him be able to do that.

Clarice ruffled Trenton's hair and smiled down at him. "I don't know what it's about," she said for perhaps the sixth time. "Maybe he just wants to show us his house." She stepped back and looked around her. The neatly trimmed hedges had been notched low to accommodate the tall, narrow windows in the front of the house. It was an oddly angular house, rather like the church in some respects but without the dark brick. Instead, it was sided with rough cedar. The chimney and front walk were made of an interesting assortment of stones, and the walk was banded on both sides by bare strips of ground that had once obviously given birth to flowers, while the beds beneath the hedges had been covered with pieces of broken bark. The house would have looked quite lovely, she thought, covered with growing ivy, flowerpots sitting to either side of the narrow, covered porch. The house could use some color, too, shutters painted a pale, soft smoky blue. She looked down at Trenton, wondering what his first impressions were of the place, and said, "You see as much or more of Bolton than I do. *You* tell *me* what it's all about."

Trenton shrugged his shoulders and grinned, but then he sobered, showing her the face of the little man he had once been, not a boy, but a somber, uncertain, *worried* little man. She felt as if her heart were being squeezed by a particularly ruthless fist, but then she reminded herself that guilt was a useless emotion. The important thing was that her little man had become a little boy at last, and she was becoming the mother she should have been all along. She smoothed his hair with her hand.

"What's bothering you, son?" she asked gently. The relief in his eyes told her that she had done and said the right thing.

He shrugged again, gazing up at her with the large, vulnerable eyes of a hopeful child. "Mom," he said, "do you like Bolt as much as I do?"

She sensed a loaded question, but her instincts told her that honesty was the only "safe" approach. She nodded. "Yes, I think so. Bolton's a very special man."

"Maybe he wants us to live with him," Trenton said wistfully.

There it was, the wish at the bottom of her son's questions, the source behind the anxiety and the nervousness. Alarm swept through her. It always did when she was contemplating the next step in her relationship with Bolton. Somehow, though, she was never alarmed when they were together. That meant something profound, she was sure; she just didn't know what. Dutifully, she pushed away the puzzle and concentrated on her son.

"What makes you say that? Has Bolton hinted to you that he would like that?"

Trenton looked down. "No," he admitted reluctantly. Then he looked up, hopeful again. "But he likes us, too. I know he does."

"I'm sure he does," she told Trenton reassuringly, "but that doesn't mean he wants us to live with him."

"What will you say if he does?" the boy asked her.

She had expected that question in a way but in another way, hadn't dreamed it would come. She could only give one answer. "I don't know."

It was as close to the truth as she could get. Bolton would never ask them to simply live with him, of course. What Trenton was talking about, without even knowing it, was marriage. That, if anything, was what Bolton would ask of them, *her*, and she no longer knew what she would say to that. She couldn't deny that she loved him. She loved him as certainly as she had *not* loved Trenton, Sr., but she would not regret that marriage. She could not when the best thing in her life had come from that marriage. Her son had come from that marriage. But enough misery had come of it, too, that she couldn't help feeling that she'd be awfully foolish to risk marriage again. She loved Bolton, but that didn't guarantee success, and she wanted, needed, to have control of her own life. It was as if her two greatest personal desires were diametrically opposed, and she was irritated with herself because her feelings in the matter could not be more precise.

Trenton obviously found her answer less than satisfying also, but he didn't press the subject. Instead, he glanced at the doorbell then back at his mother for permission to ring it. She nodded, and he punched the small, round button with a slightly grimy forefinger. Clarice shook her head, constantly amazed at the changes in her son. He had always been the most spotlessly clean child. She realized now that it was all part of him trying to be an adult to please his grandfather and perhaps to protect her—or had it been to take up the slack she'd left by not living up to her own responsibilities as a parent? One of them had to be an adult, after all. Well, that was all over now. She would never again abdicate her responsibilities—or surrender her independence. She simply couldn't, and yet, she loved Bolton. That was exactly the thought going through her mind when he opened the door.

His face lit up with a smile. "Hi! Come on in. I was just straightening up the place." As proof of this, he had a dust cloth slung over one shoulder.

Clarice noticed that he was dressed very casually in tennis shorts and polo shirt, white socks and athletic shoes. She noted, too, that he had a handsome pair of muscular legs. As usual, in his presence her senses seemed instantly heightened. She could smell the clean fragrances of bath soap and lemon oil furniture polish, the faint musk of shoe leather and honest perspiration, the pungency of cedar, the smoky sharpness of coffee. She could feel the almost nonexistent currents of cool air wafting through the open door and against her skin, the heat of the sun beating down onto the roof of the overhang beneath which she stood, the quickening of the cells of her body as they gravitated toward Bolton. She could see the gentle delineations and contours of muscle beneath the loose knit of his shirt, the tiny, crisp hairs on his arms, the lines in his knuckles, the welcome and worry in his eyes. It was this last that filled her with a premonition of foreboding.

She followed Trenton into the house. The entry was small, perhaps four-by-six feet with soft yellow wall on one side and a kind of latticework in natural wood on the other. Through the diamond-shaped openings of the lattice, she glimpsed a large room with blond woods and comfortable overstuffed furniture. The overall impression was one of comfort and coziness and handsome strength, much like Bolton himself. She liked the room even before she set foot in it, and the feeling grew as she moved among the appealing furnishings. At Bolton's urging, she and Trenton sat down on the couch while Bolton exited with his cleaning apparatus and returned moments later with a tray of ice tea in tall, frosty tumblers. Evidently he'd had it stored away in the refrigerator, for even the tray was ice-cold.

Bolton sank down into an immense chair opposite them and crossed his long, muscular legs, one ankle balanced atop one knee. He smiled at them over the rim of his glass and took a long pull of the tea. "Aaah! Nothing like cold tea on a hot day, hmm?"

"I like cola best," Trenton said. Then he gulped a drink and wiped his mouth on the back of his hand. "But this is pretty good."

Bolton's knowing, amused gaze met Clarice's, then dropped away. "It's sun tea," he said to the boy. "My mother taught me to make it. I keep a huge jar of it sitting on a tree stump out in the back."

"No way!" Trenton exclaimed, clearly intrigued.

"Honest. I have some making back there now. You can go out and see for yourself in a minute. Right now, though, I want to talk to you and your mom."

Clarice immediately tensed, the comfort and welcome of the room having momentarily overcome her sense of dread.

She swallowed tea and tried to relax. "What do you want to talk about?" she managed to ask, and immediately went back to her tea. The flavor was smooth and somehow golden, but she hardly noticed.

Bolton sat forward and set aside his glass. "Trent," he said, clasping his hands together, "I think you know that I love you." The boy nodded, his gaze steady and unflinching. Smiling gently, Bolton went on. "I think you know, too, that I love your mother."

Clarice nearly dropped her glass. She gasped and bobbled it onto the coffee table, spilling droplets of tea which she quickly mopped up with her fingertips. For all this she got no more than a smug glance from her son and no notice at all from Bolton.

"You want us to come live with you, don't you?" Trenton said matter-of-factly.

Bolton smiled. "Yes, I do."

Trenton shrugged and set his glass down beside Clarice's. "Okay by me. Does that mean you're going to marry my mother?"

"That's up to her, don't you think?" Bolton answered lightly.

"Guess so."

Clarice was gaping at the nonchalance with which her son seemed to accept the idea of moving out of the only home he had ever known. Her shock at the way the conversation was going was so great that at first she didn't even realize they were both staring at her. When she did, she was utterly dismayed. *Unfair!* she thought. It was clearly unfair of Bolton to enlist her son's approval like this! They had all but decided it between them—as if her feelings on the matter were secondary! Well, she wouldn't stand for it. This was *her* life! The thought must have communicated itself, for

Bolton sighed and turned his attention momentarily to Trent.

"Why don't you give your mom and me a few minutes of privacy?"

"Sure. Can I go out and see that tea thing now?"

"Of course." Bolton pointed at a door behind them. "Through the kitchen and out the back. You can't miss it."

Trenton ran out of the room without so much as a glance for his mother.

Clarice was angry now. How dare he take this to her son? Trenton was a child and as such his feelings were easily manipulated. It was beneath Bolton to use such tactics, and his doing so was a sore disappointment to her. She opened her mouth to say so, but he beat her to it.

"I know, I know. It was a cheap shot, but I figured it was worth a try. It was the action of a desperate man, but at least you know now that Trent has no objections to the idea."

"You couldn't discuss it with me first?"

"I thought this would be best. Obviously I was wrong. But that doesn't change anything as far as I'm concerned. I love you, and I want to marry you. I should tell you, too, that I spoke with Wallis this morning."

Clarice shot up to her feet. "You told *him* you were going to do this?"

"You see, he wanted me to stop seeing you, and when I made it clear I wouldn't, he...well, he threatened me with a scandal."

Her gaze sharpened as she stared down at him. "What scandal?"

His grin was ironic. "He says he'll tell the church that I've seduced you."

"Seduced! But it isn't true."

"No, it isn't true, and a majority of the members will know that."

"But some won't," she deduced correctly, "or they'll have doubts anyway, and that could keep you from ministering to them as you should, couldn't it?"

He inclined his head. "I don't know. Maybe. But that isn't why I want to marry you, Clarice. I meant it when I said that I love you."

He loved her. The very idea seemed to wrap around her like a pair of comforting arms, and it was true. He loved her. Somehow she knew it, and yet another idea beckoned to her. Independence. Having life her own way. Making her own decisions. Doing her own thing. Standing on her own two feet. She stepped around the end of the coffee table and strode to the window, the future and the past making the present a fierce, confusing struggle. He loved her, and she was both elated and dismayed. He loved her, and he wanted to marry her. If they did marry, he wouldn't have to worry about Wallis stirring up trouble because no one would listen to his ludicrous allegations about seduction between a legally married couple.

"I would be the rescuer this time," she muttered. But would that make any difference?

"Is that how it was?" he asked softly, much closer than she had realized.

She eased away from him. "What?"

"Is that why you married Trenton's father?" he asked. "I thought it might be because of the things you told me before. You were so young, just out of high school. Your parents had been killed in that car wreck. You had no close relatives. He rescued you, didn't he? Gave you a place to be, people to be with."

"Yes," she said, "he rescued me, and I was very grateful. I tried very hard to be the wife he wanted me to be, and I suppose I was for a while, but that didn't keep me from being bitterly unhappy."

"Did you love him, Clarice?"

Had she loved him? She knew the answer only too well. "No. And I know now that he didn't love me, either. I don't think he even wanted to love me. He just wanted a biddable, controllable wife, and God knows I was that, but I can't be that again, Bolton." She turned to face him so that he could see the earnestness of her words. "I can't be the biddable wife again."

"No one is asking you to. Maybe that was what he wanted, but it's not what *I* am asking of you. I love you, Clarice. I love you just as you are this moment. You won't be the same tomorrow, but I'll still love you, and I'll love you the day after that and the day after that and every day after as long as I live if you'll let me. I'll love you through all the changes and all the growth and all the ups and downs. I'll love you in joy and in anger and with passion and as much skill as I can manage. All I'm asking is that you love me in return. Can you do that? Do you love me, Clarice? Because if you don't—" He broke off and swallowed whatever else he might have said.

Did she love him? She wished that she didn't. How easy it would be if she did not love Bolton Charles, but wishing didn't make it so. Besides, she was through with the easy path, and it wouldn't do any good to lie to him. He would know. Just because he was Bolton, he would know. She lifted a hand to his cheek, feeling the leanness of his jaw and the faint stubble of his beard. "I love you," she said simply.

He closed his eyes in what could only be relief, and his arms came around her, pulled her against him. For a long moment, he merely held her. Her cheek was against his chest, and she listened to the strong, steady beat of his heart, trying not to think. When he curled a finger beneath her chin and tilted her head back in order to seek her mouth, she slid her arms about his waist and parted her lips beneath his. His tongue swept in to stroke her own, and his arms tightened about her.

So sweet. It was the sweetest kiss he had ever given her. Sweet and passionate, steeped in passion. He would be a skillful, ardent lover, as dedicated to her pleasure as his own, and she wanted that. Oh, how she wanted that. She grieved its loss even as she considered its gain, and tears seeped from her closed lids, slipping down her cheek to mingle their saltiness with the sweetness of his kiss.

"No, don't," he whispered, breaking away. "Please don't." He kissed her eyes and smoothed away the tears with trembling fingertips. "These aren't tears of joy, are they?"

She shook her head, stepping back out of his arms. "No. Not tears of joy."

"I don't understand."

"I know. It's just that I couldn't be a good wife for you, Bolton."

"That's nonsense."

"No, it isn't. You're a minister. People have certain expectations of a minister's wife, expectations I can't meet."

"That isn't true. You're fully capable—"

"Yes, I'm capable of meeting those expectations, but I don't *want* to meet them, Bolton. There are things I want to do for *me,* things I *have* to do for *me.*"

"Such as?"

"Such as college. I want to go to college." Only recently had she decided that was what she really wanted, but saying it aloud had suddenly made it terribly important to her. She held her breath, waiting for his reaction, but his face remained utterly impassive. Then he lifted his shoulders in an unconcerned shrug.

"All right. Fine. What college do you want to go to?"

She blinked at him. "I—I don't know."

"Well, what do you want to study, then?"

"I don't know!"

"It doesn't matter!" he said, grinning crookedly. "Study whatever you want to. It won't make any difference."

"Won't it?"

"No."

Could it be? Did it really not matter? "You make it sound so simple."

"It *is* simple," he told her. "You want to go to college. I have no problem with that, and it's not anyone else's business."

She wrinkled her brow. It *was* simple, too simple, maybe. She shook her head. "That isn't all! I want to be my own person, make my own decisions."

He gave her that shrug again. "Of course. It goes without saying. I'm asking you to be my *wife,* not my slave."

Of course. And yet... "But you aren't the only one involved!" she argued.

His brows drew together in a crease. "I'd like to know who else is involved in a marriage. There's Trent, of course, and any other children we might have. We will have other children, won't we? I'd like to have other children. Wouldn't you?"

"Yes, yes, but that's beside the point," she snapped impatiently. "I'm not talking about us and our children."

He smiled at her. It was a rather goofy smile, a wistful, knowing, silly little smile that irritated her for some reason. "You said that as if it were a fact," he explained in a husky tone.

"As if *what* were a fact?"

"Us and our children."

It did have a compellingly poignant sound to it, but she shut her eyes against it. She'd have shut her ears if she could have. "I was talking about the members of your church," she said sternly, and opened her eyes. "They're going to have certain expectations of your wife. They're going to expect her to be as involved in church activity as Carol was, and I am not Carol!"

"No, you're not Carol," he agreed gently, "and I, for one, do not want you to be Carol. Carol is gone. I love *you*. I love Clarice Revere. If anyone else is foolish enough to expect you to be Carol or even to be *like* Carol, well, we'll just have to change their expectations."

"And what if we can't do that?"

"It won't matter."

"But what if it does?"

He looked her square in the eye. "There are other churches, Clarice."

She caught her breath. "You would do that for me?"

"I would do it for us, if I felt led of God, and I'm convinced more now than ever that God means us to be together."

"You can't know that."

"I think I can, and I think you'll know it, too, before long."

"Oh, Bolton," she said, tears starting again, "why couldn't I have met you first?"

"Then you wouldn't have had Trent," he said, "and I wouldn't have had Carol, and she couldn't have taught me how to love a woman, how to love you. That's the way of it, you know. She taught me about love. I'm just beginning to realize how much she taught me about love."

"And do you think that you could teach me?" Clarice asked tremulously.

"Yes, if you'll let me, but the choice is yours. You have to choose love in order to have it, Clarice. You have to choose to be with me, to stay with me, to let me love you. You have to choose to love me. I'm not asking you to give up anything, Clarice, least of all yourself. I'm just asking you to choose." He stepped close again and slid his hands up her arms to her shoulders. "Choose me, Clarice," he whispered. "Please choose me."

"I want to," she said, sliding her arms around him and resting her head upon his shoulder. "I really want to, but I'm just not sure. I have to be sure."

He kissed the top of her head. "You will be. I'm certain."

"I hope so."

"Everything okay?"

It was Trenton, and they both turned toward him, their arms looped about one another.

"You bet," Bolton said, smiling. "I've asked your mom to marry me, and she's thinking it over."

"All right!" Trent made a fist, bent his arm at the elbow, and pumped it up and down.

"I haven't said yes, Trent," Clarice cautioned, pulling away from Bolton.

He caught her hand and linked his fingers with hers. "But I'm still working on it," he said, winking at Trent. The boy grinned, giving the idea his seal of approval. "Now, then," Bolton went on, "what did you think about my tea?"

The boy made the transition smoothly. "When do you take those brown things out?" he asked, screwing up his face.

"The tea bags? I take those out when the tea has just the right color to it."

"Is it right yet?"

"I don't know. Why don't we go check it? Then after that what do you say we start some dinner? It just so happens that I have three steaks in my refrigerator, along with the makings of a pretty fair salad and some long, juicy ears of corn."

"Yum! Corn on the cob!"

"That's a definite yes vote," Bolton declared. "What do you say, Mom?"

Clarice looked at the two of them, the people she loved most in the world, the people who loved her most, and she knew she didn't want to be with anyone else just then. Later she would think about the future. Later she would make her choice. Tonight she was just going to *be*. Tomorrow would be time enough for worrying and wondering and deciding. Tomorrow—or the day after, or...

"I'll make the salad," she said, "and Trent can clean the corn, and you..." She poked Bolton affectionately in the ribs with the long nail on her forefinger. "You can grill the steaks."

He grinned and leaned in close to kiss her cheek. "I can do a lot more than that," he whispered, "and one of these days I'll prove it."

Somehow, in that moment, she didn't doubt it. He squeezed her hand, dropped it and walked away, chattering to Trent, and still she didn't doubt. Doubt was for tomorrow—doubt and choosing.

Chapter Ten

It was a summons, plain and simple, and this time without even the veneer of polite language. He was to present himself at Revere House immediately or prepare himself to face a charge of moral turpitude. Moral turpitude. Bolton had to laugh at the phrasing. Revere was getting melodramatic in his old age. A sign of desperation? He hoped so. He very much hoped so. It would mean that Clarice was leaning in his direction, that Revere knew he was losing the battle for control. *Heavenly Father, let it be that. Please let it be that.* Revere wasn't the only one getting desperate. Give me patience, *Lord, give me wisdom.*

Bolton folded the note, using his thumbnail to crease the fine white paper with a deadly sharpness. What to do? He hated to give Revere the satisfaction of an appearance. He was not afraid of Wallis Revere. He had no reason to be afraid, and he would not appear afraid, but despite everything, Wallis was one of the flock. Wallis Revere was a wayward sheep, a stubbornly wayward sheep, more like a wayward old goat, really, but part of the flock, nonetheless, and he, Bolton, was the Shepherd's helper. He had to offer aid and guidance to Wallis Revere, even if chances were not good that Wallis would accept them. He did not want to go. He was surprised at how much he did not want to go, but he got up from the chair, walked around his desk, took his suit coat from the coat tree in the corner, put it on and walked out of the office. He passed Cora Beemis at her desk.

"Going out?" she asked distractedly, a pencil clamped between her teeth and another stuck in a clump of graying curls on the top of her head.

He grinned and nodded. "Revere House. I may be a while."

She grimaced and spat out the pencil, turning away from the quarterly calendar upon which she was working. "I thought that hand-delivered note boded ill. Somehow I didn't think it came from Trent. So it's Daniel into the lion's den, is it?"

He smiled wanly and shook his head. "More like the shepherd answering the pathetic bleat of one of the flock."

"Then the shepherd's shortsighted," Cora mused. "That's no sheep—it's a wolf in sheep's clothing."

"Maybe," he admitted, "but I have to try anyway."

"Hmph," she said, turning back to her work, "what else is new?"

Nothing, he feared, nothing at all, but he didn't say so as he left the building and walked past the sanctuary to the parking lot beyond. He had left the windows down in his sedan, and now he walked around and rolled them all up but the one on the driver's side. It was blistering hot inside, and the air from the air conditioner was every bit as sweltering as that outside. It was September, but it felt like June, late June. He loosened his tie and started up the engine. Five minutes later, buffeted by the hot wind, he felt as if he were melting. Sweat beaded his face and trickled down his spine. The air conditioner started blowing cool air about the time he pulled into the long drive of Revere House, far too late to do him any good.

He parked in the shade, rolled down all the windows again and moved up the walk toward the house. General appeared and hopped up on the doorstep as if he'd been waiting all day for Bolton to show up and let him into the house.

"Heat getting you down?" Bolton asked the cat. The cat twitched his single ear dismissively. "Just shut up and ring the bell, huh?" Bolton touched the doorbell and looked down again. "Bet you wish you had a finger." This time the cat sat down heavily upon its haunches and did not deign to twitch anything. "I have both of my ears, too," Bolton said smugly as the door opened.

It was not Teresa's cherubic face that greeted him but Clarice's pale one.

"Sweetheart, what's wrong?"

She shook her head. "I'm just so angry!" She reached out for his hand. "I'm so glad you're here."

He gripped her fingers and let her draw him inside. The cat slid in between his feet and disappeared in the direction of the kitchen. Bolton pushed the door closed with his free hand and turned back to Clarice. "Wallis?"

She nodded. "Trenton told him that we might be moving in with you."

"Ah."

"You can imagine what he made of that." She lifted her hands to his shoulders and laid her head against his chest. "Oh, Bolton, he accused me of the vilest things!"

Cold, hard anger swept through him. His chest heaved. His hands tightened into fists. "Where is he?" he said through his teeth.

"The study. But wait, Bolton. I haven't told you all of it. When I explained that you had asked me to marry you, he went a little crazy. He threw me out of his study, and then he sent Teresa's nephew with that note. I told him that if he wanted to speak with you to pick up the telephone and call you, but as usual he ignored me. Then, just a few minutes ago, I heard him talking to someone else on the phone. I don't know who it was, but Wallis was still very angry. I'm frightened, Bolton. He's going to hurt himself."

"Or someone else," Bolton murmured.

"His health is precarious. He could have a stroke."

Bolton closed his eyes and tamped down his anger. She was right, of course. He swallowed, forcing himself to put aside feelings of protectiveness and proprietorship where Clarice was concerned. He had no right to those feelings— yet. Besides, he had come as a minister, not as a lovesick swain. He took a deep breath. "I'll talk to him," he said.

She dropped her hands to his and squeezed. "Thanks. I knew I could count on you."

Tender feelings flooded him, and he smiled down at her. "Always."

She turned and led him past the wide, sweeping staircase to the corridor beyond. When they reached the study door, Bolton held her back with a hand clamped down on her arm and stepped up to the door himself. He rapped sharply, just once, opened the door and stepped inside. Wallis was sitting in the center of the room before the cold fireplace, his gnarled hands upon the wheels of his chair. He lifted his long chin and looked down his nose at Bolton, green eyes flashing, mouth set smugly.

"You're reaching mighty high, aren't you, Reverend, for a small-town preacher?"

That was a curious statement, so curious that Bolton decided Clarice was right. Wallis had gone a little crazy. He adopted a leisurely pose, hands sliding into pants pockets. "Your daughter-in-law is concerned about you, Wallis," he said evenly. "Perhaps we should call your physician."

Wallis chuckled. "Call anyone you like. It won't make any difference. There's nothing wrong with me, nothing wrong with my mind, at any rate. You're the one who didn't think things through very clearly."

Bolton frowned. Something was going on here that he hadn't quite figured out yet. "I don't understand, Wallis. What is it that I didn't think through?"

"The purse strings," Wallis informed him, smugness dripping from every syllable.

"What purse strings, Wallis?"

"What purse strings!" the old man scoffed. He seemed almost jolly and very pleased with himself. His grin was so wide and his face so lean that he looked like nothing so much as a leering cadaver.

Bolton felt a prickle of warning. "You're not making sense, Wallis. I think I should come back when you're more yourself."

The old man put back his head and laughed heartily. "You thought she had money of her own, didn't you?" he said, chuckling.

Bolton cocked his head, understanding beginning to dawn. *Purse strings. Money of her own. When I explained that you had asked me to marry you, he went a little crazy.* Bolton felt the first stirrings of his anger rising again. "You think I'm after your money, don't you?"

Wallis cackled. "Aren't you? Well, you aren't going to get it. Not a cent. My son left her nothing. He left everything to the boy, and I control that." He pulled himself up proudly. "I talked to my lawyer, and he assures me I can do what I will with the stipend she so treasures. So as of now, it goes into annuities for the boy. It'll make him a fair nest egg one day, but *she* has nothing. All she can bring you is an extensive but rather dull wardrobe."

Bolton shook his head and reached out a hand to Clarice as she stepped up next to him.

"He had nothing to leave me," she said bitterly, "because you gave him nothing and allowed him to acquire nothing. You wanted him tied to you, and you used your purse strings to do it! Well, you won't do the same to me. I can't be bought like you bought him!"

"My son loved me!" Wallis declared.

"Your son didn't love anyone," she answered quietly, her voice trembling, "not even himself. He didn't know *how* to love."

"That's a lie!"

"That's the truth, and you know it, and it's eating you alive because you're the one to blame!"

"No!"

The old man had gone white, his hands gripping the wheels of his chair so tightly that the blood vessels standing out in relief on their backs seemed ready to burst. For the first time, Bolton saw pain clouding those emerald eyes. It was true. What Clarice had said was true. Whether Wallis wanted to admit it or not, he felt great guilt concerning his son. Suddenly Bolton's every sympathetic instinct quickened. To be old and crippled and alone with such guilt, such overwhelming guilt. He had once heard hell described as the complete separation from love. To be totally without love— the very thought chilled Bolton, but the next instant he was warmed with the certainty that he would never know such a fate. And neither did Wallis have to, if only he could be made to understand.

Bolton stepped close and went down on his haunches next to Wallis's chair. "We all make mistakes," he said gently, "but God is quick to forgive when we ask."

"Ask for your own shortcomings, Reverend," the old man said with a sneer, "and while you're confessing, you might consider your motives in this marriage. Escaping scandal, greed—not a pretty picture."

Bolton sighed. "There is no scandal to escape, Wallis. That's nothing more than a product of your imagination. And as for the other, money has nothing to do with my asking Clarice to marry me. As far as I'm concerned, she can come to me with nothing more than the clothes on her back, she and Trenton."

"Never!" the old man vowed.

Bolton shook his head and slowly pushed up to his full standing height. "You can't stop us, Wallis. The decision is Clarice's, no one else's."

"That's right," Wallis said, lifting his chin and fixing his bright eyes on his daughter-in-law. "The decision is Clarice's. So you decide, girl. But keep this in mind. That little bit of money his daddy left him isn't all you'll be taking from your son if you marry without my blessing. You'll be taking this house from him, a fortune, a name that means something in this town. You listening to me, girl? Do you understand what I'm saying to you? I'll disinherit him. I'll see to it that he never gets one red penny if you take my grandson away from me."

Bolton stared at the old man, unable to believe what he'd heard. Disinherit Trent? His own grandson? He shook his head, appalled, stunned. He turned to look at Clarice, and his heart plummeted to the soles of his feet. She looked as if she'd been slapped, her eyes wide and shimmering, her mouth slightly ajar, skin colorless and dull. *To live without love,* he thought, wondering which of them he felt sorriest for, her or himself.

Clarice blinked and dragged a breath through her mouth. She could not take her eyes from Wallis. Never had she seen him so pathetic, so desperate, so *alone.* For the first time ever, she actually felt sorry for him. She closed her mouth and pushed her breath out through her nostrils, saddened and sorry. Bolton made some sort of movement on the edge of her field of vision, and she gratefully switched her gaze there. He looked stricken, anxious, and she knew suddenly what he was thinking, that he couldn't ask her to accept him if it meant Trenton giving up his inheritance. She wanted to put her arms around him and tell him that it was all right. It was all right, for what he had to offer her son far exceeded the house and the fortune and the significance of the Revere name. She had only just realized it. The love, the normalcy, the wisdom, the character, the strength—everything Bolton offered her son was priceless. Was Wallis foolish enough to think money was worth more to her son than that?

She knew suddenly that if she had been thinking about Trenton and not herself, she would already have accepted Bolton. But what about what Bolton offered her? She closed her eyes, remembering the feel of his hands and mouth, the quickness of his breath, the electricity of his touch, the strength of his desire. But it was more than that.

Controlling someone is the surest way to lose them.

Love thrives best in an atmosphere of trust and respect and confidence.

You have to choose love in order to have it, Clarice.

Carol is gone. I love you, as you are, as you will be, always.

The choice is yours.

The choice was hers, and wasn't that what freedom was all about? Wasn't that the essence of independence, the ability to choose? Even God had given His children, the freedom to choose, and it had been an act of love. She saw that now, understood it so fully. Thanksgiving flooded her soul.

I'm convinced that God means us to be together, and you will know it, too.

She did know it, knew it with a certainty she couldn't have imagined before, and a lump rose in her throat, tears swam in her eyes. She pushed them away, swallowed hard, blinked rapidly.

Tears of joy? she heard Bolton's voice saying.

"Yes, this time," she said, and then started to laugh as she realized she'd spoken aloud. The tears rolled down her cheeks, and she let them. She lifted a hand, offering it to Bolton and saw his shock, then his relief, his pride, his love. He gripped her hand in his so hard she thought he would break it. She smiled. "I love you, Bolton Charles. I am honored to accept your proposal of marriage."

Such love! She had never seen such love in a man's eyes. He lifted his free hand to her cheek, and then he stepped up close and wrapped his arms around her. She laughed against his shirt front and lifted her face for his kiss.

"You're sure?" he asked quietly.

"Absolutely certain."

"What about Trent?"

"He needs a father more than he needs money or anything else, and no one can be a better father to him than you."

Tears sparkled in his eyes. "Thank you!" he whispered, and at last his mouth came down on hers.

She slid her arms up and around his neck and gave as good as she got. He belonged to her. She belonged to him. Nothing else mattered in that moment. She forgot about Wallis and his threats and all her doubts and confusion, everything but Bolton—until she heard Teresa's sharp intake of breath.

"Meess Clarice!"

They broke the kiss, and both turned their heads in the direction of the door, their arms still looped about one another. Teresa had a look of sheer rapture on her face. She clapped her hands together.

"It is true, then, what the boy says? You're goin' to live with the Rev'rend?"

Clarice laughed, nodding. "We're going to get married first, of course."

"Oh, I so happy for you!" the maid gushed.

"Stop it!" Wallis demanded. "I didn't call you in here so you could wish them well. I want my grandson. Get him in here."

Her joy dampened a bit, Clarice glanced at Bolton. His face had gone hard. He pulled her arms from about his neck and folded her hand inside his.

"I think we should leave Trent out of this," he said sternly. "He's only a boy. He doesn't need all this acrimony."

Wallis's smile was sly. "Worried, Preacher? Afraid the boy will choose me?"

"You're not going to ask that of him, Wallis. I won't permit it. He should be able to love both of us and not feel guilty about it."

Clarice laid a hand upon his shoulder. "It's all right," she said softly, resigned to what was coming. Bolton scowled, looking for a moment as if he would argue, but then Trent was there, having run ahead of Teresa, his eager face shining up at them.

"Hi, Bolt!"

"Hi, pal. How's it going?"

Trent sent a look sideways to his grandfather. "Everybody's mad, aren't they?"

Bolton shook his head and went down on one knee. "No, son, not at you. We all love you, you know, and that's not going to change."

Trent nodded and glanced up at his mother. "Are we going to live with Bolt?"

She smoothed his hair with one hand, the other clamped tightly in Bolton's. "Yes. Does that please you?"

He smiled and threaded an arm around Bolton's neck. "Sure. But what about Grandpa?"

She glanced at Wallis, noted his gloating expression, and opened her mouth to speak, but Bolton beat her to it.

"You can see your grandfather anytime you want," he said. "We can visit here, or he can visit us, whichever. In the meantime, he'll have Teresa here to take care of him."

"I won't let them take you from me!" the old man snapped, and the boy turned toward him.

"Don't be upset, Grandpa," Trenton said gently. "It'll be all right."

"Of course it will." Wallis beckoned him closer, and Trenton slowly complied, less from reluctance than uncertainty. "Now you listen to me," Wallis said, when Trenton was standing beside the wheelchair, his hand on the armrest. "You're a Revere. Your place is here, not with the Reverend Charles. Do you understand me?"

Trenton frowned and looked to his mother.

"It's okay, honey. He can't stop us. We can go anywhere we want to go, live anywhere we want to live. We have that right."

Trenton nodded and turned pitying eyes upon his grand-father. "Maybe you could come, too. I don't think Bolt would mind."

"Never!" Wallis declared, his knotted hand banging down upon the armrest.

"I'll come visit you, then," Trent vowed a little desper-ately.

"No, you don't understand!" Wallis said sharply. "You don't have to go. You can stay here with me."

"But, Mom—"

"You don't need her! She's weak. She'll make you weak, if you let her!"

"Weak!" Bolton exclaimed hotly. "Do you think a weak woman could have stayed here all these years and put up with you? The whole world should be so weak!"

"Rubbish!"

"Truth!" Bolton retorted. "You've done everything in your power to make her dependent on you, to beat her down and keep her down, but you'll notice she's standing on her own two feet! She's making her own decisions, living her own life as *she* sees fit and asking no one's permission, least of all yours!"

"She should be grateful!"

"For what? Living? Not to you! Maybe for being made a virtual prisoner in her own home, for being ignored, un-loved, unappreciated, stripped of her rights and dreams. Is that what you had in mind, Wallis? Is that what you think she ought to be grateful to you for? Because that's what you tried to do to her!"

"No! I've only tried to do what was best for everyone!"

"Have you?" Bolton demanded. "Are you actually ca-pable of thinking beyond what's best for *you*, Wallis? If so, I haven't seen any evidence of it, yet."

The old man, for once, was speechless. Whether from despair or anger, Clarice couldn't tell. She knew only that he looked stricken, beaten, the sparkle of those green eyes strangely dimmed. She clutched Bolton's hand and bit her lip, so filled with pity for Wallis on one hand that she regretted every unkind thought or word and so overwhelmed with love for Bolton on the other that she could no longer understand her own doubts. He seemed to know her better than she knew herself, to understand so fully what she had only recently come to poorly grasp. He was right. She was *not* weak. She knew that much now. However foolish she may have been, however frightened, she was not a weakling. Even Wallis saw that now and bent the force of his will on the only truly helpless one of them.

"You don't have to go with them!" he declared, grabbing his grandson by the shoulders.

"But I want to go, Grandpa," Trenton said gently, his eyes very large and frightened.

"You don't mean that!" the old man rasped. "You'd rather be here."

"No, Grandpa."

"This is the only home you've ever known. Why would you want to leave it?"

Trenton turned his big eyes on Bolton and his mother. "I should be with them."

"But he's *not* your father!" the old man insisted. "Your father was Trenton, Sr."

"I know," Trenton said with all the wisdom of a child, "but he's in heaven. Bolt's here."

The old man seemed to crumble inwardly at that. His hands fell away and curled like dried leaves at his sides. "I won't permit it, Trenton," he said, but even he knew that it was a last, hopeless attempt destined to fail.

"I'm sorry, Grandpa," Trenton replied in a voice so small and aching that Clarice and Bolton both reached out to him.

"It's all right, son," she assured him gently. "You've nothing to apologize for. You've done nothing wrong."

"I don't want him to be sad," Trenton said, leaning back his head to look up at her.

"None of us wants him to be sad," Bolton said in a strong voice. "When he comes to understand that, he'll be happier."

Trent looked doubtfully at the crumpled form of his grandfather. His head was bowed, his gnarled hands at his temples, his shoulders slumped.

Bolton tightened his hand on the boy's shoulder comfortingly. "Listen, Trent, just because you won't be living here doesn't mean he isn't still your grandfather. You still love him, don't you?"

"Yes."

"Of course, you do, and you should. No matter what he does or says or thinks, he is your grandfather, and you should go on loving him. But it's not always easy to love, Trent, especially when people disappoint us or disagree with us or hurt us in some way. The thing is, you see, love is a choice—one we must make over and over again. That way, even if we must sometimes do difficult things, even if we make one another unhappy at times, we can go on loving. I want you to understand this now, Trent, because I want you to know that I *choose* to love you and your mother—and your grandfather. I will *always* choose to love you. That's my promise to you." He looked at Clarice, his eyes shining. "To all of you. No matter what." He looked down at the boy again and said, "Your grandfather needs to know that you love him, Trent, and that you always will."

"No matter what," the boy added solemnly.

Bolton smiled. "No matter what." He sidestepped so that he stood shoulder to shoulder with Clarice, his hand clasping hers still as if he meant never to let go, and together they watched as *their* son—for he was as surely Bolton's son in spirit as he was hers in flesh—stepped tentatively forward until he stood at his grandfather's elbow.

Wallis turned his head away, but Trenton didn't falter. He stepped up close to the chair and leaned far forward, settling his arms about the old man's neck. Very carefully he turned his head and laid it upon Wallis's shoulder. He said not a word, neither did he move again, until that frail shoulder began to shake with the force of emotion too long buried. Then Trenton's small, oddly strong hand began to gently, rhythmically pat that thin neck. After a moment, a small, pathetic whimper came from the old man, and then he threw his arms around the boy and pulled him tight against him, sobbing openly.

Clarice closed her eyes and laid her head against Bolton's shoulder to wait it out. She didn't know how long they stood there. It could have been a minute or an hour before the old man began to pull himself together. He dried his face, and his chin went up at a familiar, imperious angle. He ignored her and Bolton, and Clarice knew that he would probably never discuss what had just happened with either of them, that he would never say a word of gratitude to the one man who had taught them all so much about loving, and that it didn't matter, that she could forgive and love in a way she'd not even known possible before.

"You...you must come and see me often," he said to the boy. "W-we'll talk. W-we'll do...whatever grandfathers and grandsons do together. I'm not sure I know what that is, but we'll find out, never fear. A-and we'll remember your father together. We—I owe him that much."

Trenton nodded, an arm resting lightly across his grandfather's shoulders. Wallis reached up and patted that hand. It was the most impulsively affectionate gesture Clarice had ever seen him make, a minor miracle, to her mind.

"I hear you're quite the baseball player," Wallis said, and Trenton smiled.

"Do you like baseball, Grandpa?"

"Can't say that I do, but I want to hear all about it, anyway."

Bolton tugged on her hand, nodded toward the door and drew her quietly from the room. "Let them talk a while," he whispered as they tiptoed down the corridor. "I think we've all reached an understanding. It won't hurt to leave them alone for a bit."

"How did you know?" she asked, swinging around the end of the banister to the stairway.

"Know what?"

"What to say to Wallis. I mean, what to say to Trenton in front of Wallis."

"I didn't."

"I'm supposed to believe that was just dumb luck?" she asked, stepping up onto the bottom step and turning to face him.

He shook his head. "Oh, no. I don't believe in luck. I believe in the Divine Hand of Providence. I believe in faith and truth. I believe in pearls of wisdom generously dispensed by a loving Father. I believe God works in mysterious, unfathomable ways sometimes. I believe love is a miracle that we fail to appreciate as we should."

"Not anymore," she said softly, sliding her arms about his neck. "Not now."

He leaned into her, his forehead against her chest, his nose resting between her breasts. "Did I say that I believe in a generous, loving God who blesses us beyond all reason or understanding?''

She smiled against the crown of his head. "Something like that."

He tightened his arms about her waist. "You smell so good."

"Mmm, so do you."

"You won't make me wait long, will you?" he asked, lifting his head and stepping up onto the bottom stair with her, so that she stood between his legs, their bodies pressed tightly together. "I want you so much. I want you beside me—and in my bed—for the rest of my life."

She turned her face up to his, eyes glowing, arms locked about him. "I won't make either of us wait long. Is tomorrow soon enough?"

"Yesterday wouldn't have been soon enough," he said softly. "Forever won't be long enough. I want to explore with you all the mysterious, miraculous aspects of love. I want to get to know and understand every one—starting with the physical ones, if you please."

"I please very much," she murmured, feeling as if her heart might lift right out of her chest and float heavenward.

He grinned. "I know." And bending his head, he kissed her.

It was a no-holds-barred kind of kiss, with nothing held back, everything promised and more to come. Blatantly sensual, provocatively seductive and human, oh, so human.

"Eeew," said a small, familiar voice that effectively broke the kiss. "Are you guys gonna do that from now on?"

Clarice glanced at Bolton and started to pull away, only to feel his arms tighten about her.

He looked down upon the boy, a smile twitching at one corner of his mouth. "Yes," he said simply, flatly, "from now on."

Trenton stared at them, then hitched up one shoulder. "Okay," he said, as if he couldn't figure out for the life of him why but was willing to indulge their silliness anyway. He turned and headed for the door, at which point the cat appeared, his small, pink tongue flicking over his snout as if he'd just taken it from a saucer of milk, which he probably had. "Come on, General Tom. I want to get my trucks from the sand bed. We're getting a new house," Trent said, "and a whole new family and a church and everything! There's even a stump and a jar for tea and . . ." He went on, but the closing door muffled the rest. General didn't seem too impressed, but then why should he be? He was a cat and as such had no interest in tea or parents or grandparents or siblings or love or anything except his saucer of milk and his dignity.

Bolton chuckled and turned his attention back to the woman in his arms. "It seems we've been given permission to continue."

"Then by all means," she said, loving him with every fiber of her being and exulting in the image of that carefree little boy who had just left them to babble to his cat in the most complacent fashion about the most miraculous, wondrous things, "get on with it."

And he did. Oh, he did.

* * * * *

HE'S MORE THAN
A MAN, HE'S
ONE OF OUR

DADDY'S ANGEL
Annette Broadrick

With a ranch and a houseful of kids to care for, single father Bret Bishop had enough on his mind. He didn't have time to ponder the miracle that brought lovely Noelle St. Nichols into his family's life. And Noelle certainly didn't have time to fall in love with Brett. She'd been granted two weeks on earth to help Brett remember the magic of the season. It should have been easy for an angel like Noelle. But the handsome rancher made Noelle feel all too much like a woman....

Share the holidays with Bret and his family in Annette Broadrick's *Daddy's Angel*, available in December.

Fall in love with our **Fabulous Fathers!**

Take 4 bestselling love stories FREE

Plus get a FREE surprise gift!

Special Limited-time Offer

Mail to Silhouette Reader Service™

3010 Walden Avenue
P.O. Box 1867
Buffalo, N.Y. 14269-1867

YES! Please send me 4 free Silhouette Romance™ novels and my free surprise gift. Then send me 6 brand-new novels every month, which I will receive months before they appear in bookstores. Bill me at the low price of $1.99* each plus 25¢ delivery and applicable sales tax, if any.* That's the complete price and—compared to the cover prices of $2.75 each—quite a bargain! I understand that accepting the books and gift places me under no obligation ever to buy any books. I can always return a shipment and cancel at any time. Even if I never buy another book from Silhouette, the 4 free books and the surprise gift are mine to keep forever.

215 BPA AJH5

Name	(PLEASE PRINT)	
Address	Apt. No.	
City	State	Zip

This offer is limited to one order per household and not valid to present Silhouette Romance™ subscribers. *Terms and prices are subject to change without notice. Sales tax applicable in N.Y.

USROM-93R   ©1990 Harlequin Enterprises Limited

UNDER THE MISTLETOE

*Where's the best place to find love
this holiday season?* UNDER THE MISTLETOE,
*of course! In this special collection, some of
your favorite authors celebrate the joy of the
season and the thrill of romance.*

Available in December from

Silhouette
ROMANCE™

SRXMAS

MEN MADE IN AMERICA

Fifty red-blooded, white-hot, true-blue hunks
from every State in the Union!

Look for MEN MADE IN AMERICA! Written by some
of our most poplar authors, these stories feature fifty of
the strongest, sexiest men, each from a different state in
the union!

Two titles available every other month at your favorite
retail outlet.

In November, look for:

STRAIGHT FROM THE HEART by Barbara Delinsky
(Connecticut)
AUTHOR'S CHOICE by Elizabeth August (Delaware)

In January, look for:

DREAM COME TRUE by Ann Major (Florida)
WAY OF THE WILLOW by Linda Shaw (Georgia)

You won't be able to resist MEN MADE IN AMERICA!

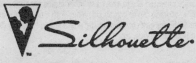

Relive the romance...
Harlequin and Silhouette
are proud to present

A program of collections of three complete novels by the most-requested
authors with the most-requested themes. Be sure to look for one volume each
month with three complete novels by top-name authors.

In September: **BAD BOYS** Dixie Browning
Ann Major
Ginna Gray
No heart is safe when these hot-blooded hunks are in town!

In October: **DREAMSCAPE** Jayne Ann Krentz
Anne Stuart
Bobby Hutchinson
Something's happening! But is it love or magic?

In December: **SOLUTION: MARRIAGE** Debbie Macomber
Annette Broadrick
Heather Graham Pozzessere
Marriages in name only have a way of leading to love....

Available at your favorite retail outlet.

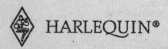

SILHOUETTE.... Where Passion Lives

Don't miss these Silhouette favorites by some of our most popular authors!
And now, you can receive a discount by ordering two or more titles!

Silhouette Desire®

#05751	THE MAN WITH THE MIDNIGHT EYES BJ James	$2.89	☐
#05763	THE COWBOY Cait London	$2.89	☐
#05774	TENNESSEE WALTZ Jackie Merritt	$2.89	☐
#05779	THE RANCHER AND THE RUNAWAY BRIDE Joan Johnston	$2.89	☐

Silhouette Intimate Moments®

#07417	WOLF AND THE ANGEL Kathleen Creighton	$3.29	☐
#07480	DIAMOND WILLOW Kathleen Eagle	$3.39	☐
#07486	MEMORIES OF LAURA Marilyn Pappano	$3.39	☐
#07493	QUINN EISLEY'S WAR Patricia Gardner Evans	$3.39	☐

Silhouette Shadows®

#27003	STRANGER IN THE MIST Lee Karr	$3.50	☐
#27007	FLASHBACK Terri Herrington	$3.50	☐
#27009	BREAK THE NIGHT Anne Stuart	$3.50	☐
#27012	DARK ENCHANTMENT Jane Toombs	$3.50	☐

Silhouette Special Edition®

#09754	THERE AND NOW Linda Lael Miller	$3.39	☐
#09770	FATHER: UNKNOWN Andrea Edwards	$3.39	☐
#09791	THE CAT THAT LIVED ON PARK AVENUE Tracy Sinclair	$3.39	☐
#09811	HE'S THE RICH BOY Lisa Jackson	$3.39	☐

Silhouette Romance®

#08893	LETTERS FROM HOME Toni Collins	$2.69	☐
#08915	NEW YEAR'S BABY Stella Bagwell	$2.69	☐
#08927	THE PURSUIT OF HAPPINESS Anne Peters	$2.69	☐
#08952	INSTANT FATHER Lucy Gordon	$2.75	☐

	AMOUNT	$ _____
DEDUCT:	10% DISCOUNT FOR 2+ BOOKS	$ _____
	POSTAGE & HANDLING	$ _____
	($1.00 for one book, 50¢ for each additional)	
	APPLICABLE TAXES*	$ _____
	TOTAL PAYABLE	$ _____
	(check or money order—please do not send cash)	

To order, complete this form and send it, along with a check or money order for the total above, payable to Silhouette Books, to: *In the U.S.*: 3010 Walden Avenue, P.O. Box 9077, Buffalo, NY 14269-9077; *In Canada*: P.O. Box 636, Fort Erie, Ontario, L2A 5X3.

Name: _____

Address: _____ City: _____

State/Prov.: _____ Zip/Postal Code: _____

*New York residents remit applicable sales taxes.
Canadian residents remit applicable GST and provincial taxes.

SBACK-OD

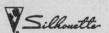